D0324377

FOOL'S
COACH

AN EVANS NOVEL OF THE WEST

RICHARD S. WHEELER

M. EVANS & COMPANY, INC. NEW YORK

For Michael and Kathleen Gear

Library of Congress Cataloging-in-Publication Data

Wheeler, Richard S.

Fool's Coach / Richard S. Wheeler.
p. cm. — (An Evans novel of the West)
ISBN 0-87131-560-2
I. Title. II. Series.
PS3573.H4345F66 1989 89-1262
813′.54—dc19

M. Evans and Company, Inc.
216 East 49 Street
New York, New York 10017

Manufactured in the United States of America

9 8 7 6 5 4 3 2 1

Author's Note

Some of the characters in this story are historical. With minor exceptions, all of the road agents were real people, as well as the merchants Dance and Pfouts.

In late December 1863, George Ives was found guilty of murder by an informal miners' court and hanged. At the same time vigilantes organized at Paris Pfouts's store in Virginia City, along with similar groups in Nevada City and Bannack City, and within two months broke the power of the road agents, trying and hanging a great many of them. Among the first to be hanged was the leader of the road agents, Sheriff Henry Plummer, who had been elected informally by the miners—there being little organized government at the time—in May 1863. The noose tightened around Plummer's neck on January 10, 1864.

During 1863, Bannack and Virginia City were a part of Idaho Territory, and not until the next year was Montana Territory organized. That story, one of the most absorbing in the chronicles of the early West, has been told and retold in history, biography, and fiction.

Chapter One

They jumped Aristotle Scrimshaw on a cold November night down in Alder Gulch, just above Virginia City. It was moonless and breezy, or he would have seen or heard them, but he didn't, and the first thing he knew cold steel jammed into his back and a rough hand clamped over his holstered Navy.

Two of them, it turned out. Aristotle was not a particularly strong or large man, but years of relentless placer mining had toughened him, and he struggled hard. His elbow caught one of them in the gut, and his fist landed hard on the other's left arm, and then they wrestled him to earth.

The gun in his back was a ruse and he knew it. They had no intention of killing him.

"Hold steady, you son of a bitch," snapped one, "or it's good-bye."

Aristotle fell flat on his back. They didn't have his legs pinioned, so he rammed a knee up, caught one of them hard, and Aristotle heard an explosion of breath and smelled rotgut.

One of them cracked him then with the butt of a revolver, and

Aristotle's brain exploded into shooting stars. They dug into his buffalo-hide coat first, pawing at his flannel shirt pocket, and found the letter.

"Here she is," said one.

They rolled him over and dug into his pockets for his poke, and got that, too, yanking the small cowhide pouch from his corduroy britches.

"It's light," said the other, disappointed. "But it don't matter."

The one pinning Aristotle's shoulders laughed.

"If you tell anyone about this, Scrimshaw, you're dead. We're watching you every minute, and we got big ears everywhere."

Then they vanished, the scuff of boots harsh in the moonless void.

Aristotle Scrimshaw's skull clanged like a horse trolley and his vision doubled. Every star turned into two stars, and two Big Dippers hung in the north. He lay quietly on his back, not yet ready to get up, but his mind already at work.

The poke wasn't worth much—he rarely carried over ten dollars of dust at night. But that letter worried him. It would tell them what they needed to know. It had arrived in Virginia City that day by stage from the Overland Trail far to the south. He'd picked it up at Stuart and Dance's, the new log mercantile up the hill, where one could find a little of everything from harness to barrels of flour—when the erratic freight trains brought it.

He heard footfalls, and Aristotle quietly clawed at his holster, but it was empty. He lay still on his back, and the footsteps drifted by and vanished in the night. He wanted to get up, but any movement made his head throb. He lay a half mile from his log cabin, built into the cliff on his best claim. The night grew chilly, but he was in no hurry.

The letter had come from Annette, the first he'd received from her since the fall of 'sixty-two, and only the second in the two years since he'd left her in Wisconsin, along with Margaret and Thompson, his girl and boy, on the farm near Eagle. It had been written in August, and the news was all bad. Thompson, barely fourteen years old, had military, or galloping, tuberculosis and grew weaker daily. His little girl, his sunny Margaret, had had the ague, but seemed better. That wasn't the end of it, either. The farm might go under. The Husbandmen's Bank of Eagle had already confiscated the dairy herd, and unless full payments were made on the small mortgage, the bank would foreclose January 1, 1864.

"Fly home, Aristotle, fly home before it is too late. I love you and need you and want my arms around you, my love," Annette had concluded.

He had read it three times next to Stuart and Dance's hissing potbellied stove, oblivious of the other miners and townsmen who were clamoring for their mail. If there had been eyes upon him, he wasn't aware of it.

Odd, he thought. He had left everything in good shape, a small dairy herd for cash, fields of grass his son could easily mow and windrow and stack into piles, chickens, hogs, vegetable gardens, and much more that would see them through until he returned. But the boy's consumption had changed all that. Now he had to get back. Between Virginia City, Idaho, and southern Wisconsin there lay no direct route, and whether he followed the Missouri River or rode overland, he had a two-thousand-mile journey before him.

With gold.

He sat up now, nauseous but able to walk. He studied the grass, looking for his Navy revolver, hoping to pick up a star glint upon cold metal, but he saw none. The road agents had it, then. They got most everything in Alder Gulch that wasn't nailed down these days.

Aristotle felt the bump on his head gingerly, and lowered his wide-brimmed gray felt hat onto his head, and struck off up the gulch, still dizzy from the blow and too tired to be cautious. Only one thing filled his mind. He had to find some way to get out of Alder Gulch alive, and at once. Not a minute did he have to spare. Across a continent, Annette cried out to him, and his own heart cried back. He had come to the diggings to make the family fortune, escape subsistence farming, give his children a future and his wife all the comforts she had been born to.

And he'd succeeded through hard work where other men failed. He had worked a poor claim above Bannack City in 1862, and then when gold was discovered by Bill Fairweather and all the rest over in Alder Gulch in early 1863, Scrimshaw dashed east, among the first to arrive, and located on a rich gravel bar. In five months he'd panned a fortune. In the small green safe at Stuart and Dance's were pokes with his name on them, pokes filled with gold dust totaling over one hundred thousand dollars, more than any other miner had ripped out of Alder Gulch.

The road agents knew it was there, and watched him with the eye of a cyclops. Lounging roughs saw him scratching gravel at dawn, ripping gold from his rich bar, panning it at first and sluicing it whenever he found water enough, working through bad weather while the others loafed and hunkered around stoves and bought jugs. The road agents had leered while Aristotle bought up the claims of the quitters and the lazy, one by one, until he owned eleven of them. Some of these he leased on shares, but that wasn't a good arrangement, even when the other men were honest enough. The bulk of the dust that he accumulated in tiny silvery flakes and pea-sized nuggets was the harvest of his own brutal toil and intelligent digging and caution.

He lit an oil lamp in his cabin. Nothing had been disturbed. His single vision had returned and he peered at the rough shelves and his stores carefully. Nothing. They knew they wouldn't find anything here. They had seen him take his daily gain up to Stuart and Dance's by daylight seven days a week, when a man could safely walk about. They had waited and were still waiting. Well, he thought, they'd have their big chance soon. Annette's letter told them that.

His cabin was tight and carefully built, like everything that Aristotle did, and soon he felt warm. He would leave. Sell his claims and slip away. He had less than two months to get from here to there. Only one winter route lay open: he had to get to the Oregon Trail and then catch one of Ben Holladay's coaches east.

He would have preferred to catch a packet at Fort Benton and sail down the wide Missouri, but summer was long gone and with it the little packets from St. Louis that toiled their way up the vicious river to deposit their precious cargoes at Fort Benton, which was as far as they could go. Always they hurried down again, loaded with buffalo hides and beaver pelts and pilgrims returning to the states, before the spring floods vanished and left them stranded. But November had arrived and the only way out would be a cold, bone-jarring stagecoach across the plains.

Angelica Ramirez had a bad time keeping girls. Lonely miners proposed to them almost daily, and most of the girls accepted sooner or later and left the life. The Grasshopper Digs were a long way from anything. Bannack City was a crude town of log buildings and canvas and adobe huts that offered nothing to a woman beyond what friendships she could form with rough miners.

No matter what Angelica did, it wasn't enough. Her solidly built log sporting house felt comfortable and secure, and thwarted the biting winds. She made sure each girl had two rooms—one for business and the other for her private haven. She acquired good wood stoves, a Chinese cook, some novels shipped from San Francisco at great cost, carpets, and a pianoforte. She paid for occasional vacations in Salt Lake City, where they could buy good clothing from the Mormon dressmakers. But it was never enough, and the girls abandoned her regularly, usually without notice, and often within a few weeks of their arrival. Now she was shorthanded because big blond Amanda had eloped with Ansel Sturgis, who had a profitable placer claim.

She had thought that if comforts and amenities weren't enough, then money might be, so she raised her prices to ten, then fifteen, and finally twenty dollars of dust and let each girl keep half. She had sent word back east that a girl could make a fortune here in four or five months—enough to settle her for life. That brought the girls. They drifted in by stagecoach from Fort Benton and the river packets, or arrived dust-caked and weary after endless miles along the Oregon Trail. A few looked pretty, hardly any were plain, and more than a few were fresh off the immigrant boats landing in Boston and New York. Many an Irish lass had knocked on her red door, looking for quick security before settling somewhere else in the New World. Angelica, who wore only black, welcomed them all, sent a few charity cases away without employing them, and trained the others to the life.

No matter what she charged, the miners came and spilled their dust into her fine brass scales and then selected one of her Cyprians and disappeared for a while, usually a pathetic five minutes, and then reappeared, not looking her in the eye. Some lingered in the saloon afterward. Most headed for the saloon beforehand, needing a dose of spirits to nerve themselves to buy a lady. She worried most about the ones who took their time. Those were the ones who befriended the girls, courted them, and often swept them out of her place, the Red Parlor, forever, and with scarcely a good-bye.

Business was tailing off, too. Most of the miners had rushed madly to the next bonanza, Alder Gulch, and Bannack City had begun its heavy spiral downward, even though the mines prospered. Angelica didn't much care. She thought of moving her whole business to Virginia City, where she would build a fine log establishment in Daylight Gulch and keep right on. But she felt weary, and her other dream grew stronger now that she had become rich. The more she thought of San Francisco, the white city of California, still filled with so many of her own Hispanic people, the more she longed to go there. She had seen it once and loved it.

George Ives swept in, along with a blast of cold November air. He carefully closed the carmined door behind him and grinned at her while he warmed his hands in the aura of the black and silver potbellied stove.

"Evening, Angelica," he said.

She liked him. Was there ever such a one as this young man of no means with the bright eyes as azure as the sky of Santa Fe, this blond Adonis with the wild, sunny spirit and an amiable jest forever on his tongue? The girls enjoyed him, too. He hired them by the hour, treated them kindly and with good humor, and left amazing tips—greenbacks, gold dust, jewelry, or even pocket watches, sometimes with an engraved name scratched out.

"You've come for sport, George?"

"All night," he said. "I want Clarissa."

"Bueno." Angelica smiled and nodded. The raven-haired tall square girl sat at the pianoforte in the parlor. Ives sat down beside her, slid an arm around her shoulder, and whispered something. She smiled and the pair of them strolled through the gilded doorway into the quiet, dark, private part of the building that seemed to exude mysteries.

Angelica had not requested payment, but Clarissa would do it. That was a rule—always money in advance. If the customers would not pay it, then her glitter-eyed brown giant, Alfonso, would eject them. She watched them go, her brown eyes following Ives through the doorway.

He was one of them, she thought. One of the reasons she could not easily leave here, leave the business, return to being her real self, return to being the respectable woman she had been. She couldn't prove it, of course, but *Dios!* everyone knew. Nothing of value ever left Bannack or Virginia City in safety. Not even the mule skinners and bullwhackers escaped, although the camps depended on them for food and hardware, guns and ammunition and gold pans and nails.

The road agents swarmed everywhere, and had eyes and ears in every store and saloon, and maybe even here in her own house. No one escaped their surveillance. Let a miner try to slip away in the night, and he'd be found dead, or he would vanish from the world. Let one of her girls head back where she came from, carrying her new fortune, and she'd be robbed and made to suffer indignities. She knew of no one of her girls who had made it out, to Salt Lake or Fort Benton, with her wealth intact. And she knew of two score men who had stopped at the Red Parlor for a last fling before leaving Bannack City or the Alder Gulch digs, only to be murdered hours later in some obscure gulch in this terrible wilderness, robbed of all they possessed including life. On those last nights she had taken their dust, given them a good time, and then said *adiós,* knowing their fate.

Murdered by parties unknown. And known. Like George Ives. He scarcely bothered to hide it. He claimed to have a small ranch near Virginia City—and spent a thousand a month. He had no placer claims and no other known business. He lived in a small log house above the Alder Gulch and surveyed his world with mocking blue eyes.

Sometime, Angelica thought, those bright blue eyes gazed too long on her, watched her measure the dust on her brass scale and pour it into a small canvas sack, watched her carry these sacks into her private rooms and the strongbox there. So far they hadn't robbed her. Alfonso hovered close, and she herself was never without a derringer on her person. They rarely robbed in Bannack City or Virginia City anyway, preferring to catch their victims out where there were no witnesses. Along the roads and trails they waylaid travelers almost daily, usually masked by bandanas and blankets, and armed with sawed-off shotguns and twin Colt Navies, and perhaps a knife. And if the victims did not instantly raise their hands, they were as good as dead.

But men read voices as well as faces, so the identities of many of the road agents became known or suspected. Angelica knew. She paid her girls bonuses to ask questions, so she knew a lot more than most people. It frightened her, all that she knew, and kept her rooted in her small, safe world of the Red Parlor.

Clarissa returned alone briefly, her lounging robe loose about her and half undone, and her lips loose and kissed. "Here," she said, dropping grubby green bank notes into Angelica's hands. It was a hundred dollars in tens and twenties, a small fortune.

"I will record it," she said to Clarissa. "You are getting very rich very fast."

But the dark, square girl had gone. Angelica eyed the grimy greenbacks with a certain pleasure. Mr. Lincoln's wartime money seemed to bleed value almost daily and would buy forty percent less than gold, but it was light and easily hidden in small things. Gold dust lay heavy and gave everything an unnatural weight. Yes, she thought, the greenbacks weren't like gold. But it would be better to escape here with some of her fortune than with none. The greenbacks might be artfully hidden in the silk linings of portmanteaus and the hems of dresses and might go unnoticed, while every last ounce of hidden gold would be rooted out within ten miles of this camp.

She straightened the greenbacks thoughtfully. Maybe she'd heat up her flatiron on the stove and iron them so they'd hide better when her moment came. Funny, she thought, how she adored George Ives, who might at any time kill her for her gold. If he had any idea how much she had, he would risk it. There weren't many Anglos she adored, but he was one, always joking, always happy, always on edge.

But some of Ives's friends frightened her. Buck Stinson and Ned Ray were two. Boone Helm seemed the worst, a giant of a man who seethed with some sort of inner violence and had a murderous eye. Whenever he lumbered in, she feared for her girls and set Alfonso to listening at the door, armed with a heavy Walker Colt. The sheriff himself, Henry Plummer, frequently came to sport even though he had just married. He was suave and portly and well-spoken, but wary of eye. She couldn't make up her mind about him, though some female instinct warned her always to be careful. He never stared hungrily into her private room the way Ives did, but he glanced at the strongbox there nonetheless, and swiftly peered elsewhere. But she saw it, and found herself uncertain about him.

She always greeted him cordially but with reserve, about the way he greeted her. She took his money—which he parted with reluctantly, amiably complaining about her high prices—and then queried her girls after he had left. Had he abused them? No, they always replied, he'd been gentle and polite. Once he had tried to buy her, Angelica, and when she had snapped back her answer, she saw a flash of cold death for the smallest second in his eyes, and it had frightened her.

So she didn't trust him. How she would like to read Henry

Plummer's soul! How she would like to prick him with her fine Toledo stiletto, prick his flesh until the truth bled out of this new sheriff of this vast undefined Idaho county. Prick him until that false, bland smile tumbled aside and she could see the murder and greed of him plain on his lips.

She plucked up the bills and shifted her black rebozo tighter around her ivory neck and slipped into her own overly hot quarters. Her ornate black four-poster bed had never had a man in it: she was of this life, but not a part of it, and *Dios mediante,* she'd soon escape from here forever. She eyed the black strongbox dubiously. Anyone with a little patience and a crowbar could wrench it open, she thought. And yet she would not store her gold with any merchant. She trusted no one. Inside that box rested her fortune and more—her life, her future, her every hope. She wasn't sure how much, but she knew it would amount to at least a hundred fifty thousand dollars of nuggets and dust, plus another ten thousand in currency. All in one basket, she thought. A fortune in a frail vault, and every road agent knew it was there, waiting . . . .

Impulsively she yanked the pile of bills from the iron box and pressed the new currency into the stack. On the log wall hung two daguerreotypes of her boys, Jaime and Carlos, and she could never stare at those two likenesses, made so long ago now, without a lurch of her heart. They'd be so much older. Grown men, almost. Would they even recognize her? Did they know what she did, what she had become? Would they ever understand why she had fled that madman, her husband, their father, who beat her and threatened to kill her, and used her shamefully whenever he had guzzled too much aguardiente? She had tried to take them with her, but it had gone wrong and she had fled in the night with nothing, fled into a Santa Fe winter night with blasphemies and bullets whistling by her, fled with nothing at all but a will to live, a broken body, a proud spirit, and a love of two little boys.

She took all the bills and wrapped them with butcher paper in thin packets and pasted the paper tight. From the wall she removed the portraits of Jaime and Carlos—portraits she had bribed a servant woman to smuggle to her from her husband's adobe house on Delgado Street—and pried off the pasteboard backs. There would be room. She laid packets of bills between the daguerreotypes and the pasteboard backs, and then glued everything back together. That took care of about six thousand dollars in currency. She hung the portraits back on the wall. That much, at least, would be safe. The act had been a declaration of independence. She would leave here now. Not wait another minute. But she didn't know how to smuggle six hundred pounds of gold dust past the most ruthless and murderous band of cut-throats the western wilderness had ever seen. *Madre de Dios,* it seemed too much for one poor woman, but who could she trust?

Chapter Two

Professor Randolph Figaro thought he might go south for the winter for his health. In fact, he knew that if he stayed in Virginia City, he'd soon come down with fatal perforations of approximately .44 caliber. That was a common enough disease in the new mining camp, striking randomly rich and poor, young and old. Only women seemed to escape it.

Not that he lacked protection. He carried an over-and-under derringer in the breast pocket of his fine gray swallowtail coat with the black velvet collar and lapels. A single-shot holstered on his patent leather black high-top shoes. And a spring-loaded knife strapped to his left forearm, a missile that could be catapulted from his shirtsleeve with such force that it would bury itself in the flesh of someone across the green baize table.

He had won his full professorship in the College of the Mississippi, so to speak, where he dealt faro and played poker in the fine gilded salons of the puffing packets that toiled up and down the river. Some of those in his calling pretended not to be what they were. They dressed in the most sober fashion, contriving to seem more like Baptist deacons than apostles of Lady Luck, if indeed luck had anything to do with it. But the professor had other ideas. He wore his profession plain, and not a man glanced at him but knew exactly what he was. It saved embarrassment. It also brought him a bountiful supply of women of a certain sort, women of the demimonde, not quite respectable but not the pure sporting variety either. He liked those, the easy ones who enjoyed pleasure and excitement but could not exactly be bought, at least not for one night and not for a few dollars. To be sure, Randolph Figaro bought one occasionally, but more often they simply attached themselves to him, and indeed one had become a partner for a while, shrewder than he when it came to studying the vulnerabilities of someone across the green baize.

Professor Figaro had been plying his amiable trade in Bannack City when the pell-mell rush to Virginia City drained away most of the camp in early June. It annoyed him. By mining camp standards, Bannack had become old and comfortable, solidly built of log and plank and adobe. He had a good life, rising around noon and retiring, almost always richer than the previous day, around one or two in the morning, except for the occasional all-night sessions when one or another player was determined to beat him, and rarely did.

But he knew all about these things, and a month or so after the mad rush seventy miles east to Alder Gulch, he packed up his cards after carefully shaving their worn edges once again, folded his oilcloth faro layout, paid off the saloonkeeper, Pyreen, and joined the crowd. It always took them a week or two to civilize the new place, and he was in no rush. By the time he arrived there were already two towns of sorts, Virginia City and Nevada City, and assorted others in the mushroom stage.

It never failed to amaze him that in six weeks an entire town could arise where there had been none. When he dismounted at the Alder diggings, two thousand people swarmed about, only a few of them miners with claims. The rest were teamsters, woodcutters, bakers, lawyers, doctors, saloonkeepers, teachers, land grabbers, hunters, printers, merchants, mechanics, blacksmiths, ladies of the night, builders, eatery operators, pianists, waitresses, Dutchmen, Swedes, and Germans who muttered in tongues, deserting soldiers hiring out as toughs, one church organist, some cattlemen, three sheepherders, one pig farmer, three respectable wives, stage-line operators, and even bankers and preachers. At every hand buildings burgeoned, even two-story mercantiles, and the tent saloons and tent bordellos operated around the clock at feverish pitch.

He found two long log rooming houses going up, and even before they were done the proprietors were renting cubicles barely wide enough for a narrow bed, doorless, and roofless except for canvas because the carpenters had not got around to building a roof yet. Figaro eyed them distastefully and opted against them. Nothing would be safe if stored within. Instead he wandered into a substantial new saloon built of fieldstone and mud mortar, with a puncheon floor and a rather classy mirror-backed bar that had been freighted in from somewhere. Compared to the plank-and-tree-stump outfits in ragged tents, Cyrus Churchill's establishment was high-class.

In short order, Professor Figaro worked out a deal: faro and poker out front, fifty percent of the profits to the house, plus a sleeping cot back in the storeroom, where his few possessions would be reasonably safe, especially under the watchful eye of burly, rough Churchill, who seemed no man to trifle with. And all the red-eye, popskull, and rattlesnake juice he wanted. That stuff would be free; real bourbon would cost. Churchill made that clear enough.

It turned out to be a mistake, and one he could not readily repair. Churchill's saloon had a special clientele, certain gents that Professor Figaro knew either by reputation or on sight. Between them, they poured dust lavishly, bucked the faro layout with piles of chits bought with nuggets or dust, played sloppy poker because they little cared whether they won or lost, fondled the serving doxy—Churchill had hired a hard woman to peddle his red-eye but he had no back rooms here, and he did not consider the establishment a sporting house—and never wondered where the next pinch of gold would come from.

In short, these were the road agents, though none dared say it, because such an accusation whispered in the wrong ears would result in sudden disappearance. The professor suggested blandly to Churchill that he'd prefer to set up his layout elsewhere, but Churchill would have none of it and pointedly asked why. To give a reason was to invite death, Figaro knew, so he muttered something about the storeroom being cold—and stayed.

Professor Figaro was no pilgrim, and so he took what few measures he could. He dragged his faro layout from the center of the long dark room to one mortared rock wall corner, giving him safety on two sides and sparing him surprises. And he contrived to win modestly, or even lose a bit, whenever certain of the gents at his tables looked particularly rabid. He was all ears, too, knowing how swiftly he could gather life-saving information if he smiled suavely and kept his mouth shut. One of them cheated at poker, but Randolph Figaro did nothing.

Regulars idled here, and soon enough he had their names: Whiskey Bill, Dutch John Wagner, Bob Zachary, Buck Stinson, Ned Ray, Greaser Joe Pizanthia, Clubfoot George Lane, Steve Marshland, Big Bill Bunton, Alex Carter, Bill Hunter, Haze Lyons, Jack Gallagher, Frank Parish. . . . And the one who spent whole nights in the place, George Ives, with the flashing blue eyes and ready grin.

Some nights Sheriff Plummer, over from Bannack City, seemed to headquarter at Churchill's, along with his deputies, Jack Gallagher, Buck Stinson, and Ned Ray. The other deputy, Dillingham, rarely entered the joint, the professor observed, and it made a man wonder. The place was, after a fashion, protected by the law, and that, after a fashion, pleased the professor. In a matter of days his purse had fattened by two thousand. Within a fortnight he was four thousand ahead, even after carefully splitting the take with Cyrus Churchill, who watched with hard eyes and virile puffs of a dog-turd-colored Havana.

Around the professor Virginia City mushroomed, but he saw

little of it. He slept by day and worked by lanternlight. The Mechanical Bakery started up over on Wallace Street. Morier's Saloon, a more respectable one than Churchill's, opened its doors. Mercantiles opened to trade. While Randolph Figaro slept, Virginia City stirred to life. And even as this amazing wilderness metropolis sprang to life, death stalked its citizens. Fifty, a hundred, two hundred corpses lined the seventy-odd miles from Bannack City to Virginia City.

Randolph Figaro's troubles began one late October night when the mountain air felt nippy and the hazy lamplit saloon seemed a particularly amiable haven against the cold wilderness outside. A larger crowd gathered in Churchill's than he had ever seen, people in from Bannack, including Sheriff Plummer and a coarse, florid fellow named Ned Bunton. Both of them were at his table now, playing desultorily and watching the professor pull cards out of the casebox in the rhythm of the game: loser, winner, loser, winner. Randolph Figaro kept his own cases. Oddly, no one else sat at the layout, though the place was packed.

The jowly sheriff bet the king to lose, dropping five chips on the spade king painted on the oilcloth and coppering the bet. But the king won, and Figaro raked in the chips.

"You have all the luck, professor," Plummer said amiably.

Figaro nodded.

"Where're you from?" the sheriff asked.

It was not a question customarily asked in the West, and the novelty of it lifted Figaro's eyes to those of Plummer. "Why, suh, the Pike's Peak districts."

"And before that, the Confederacy. Lots of fellows here escaping the war," Plummer said lazily.

Bunton won a small pile of counters and belched happily. Plummer lost again. Randolph Figaro watched and waited.

"A gent like you needs a proper bank," Plummer said. "Here you are, skinning away the dust of these hard working innocents, listening to their talk, nodding and saying nary a word, and these gents know nothing about you."

"I know nothing about you all," said the professor.

"You need a bank, and we happen to be opening up one—where your winnings will be safe. Mr. Bunton here is a pioneer rancher over near Bannack—Rattlesnake Ranch. Stage stop, you know. He and I have been thinking, here you are, professor, a stranger in these parts and without friends. You need friends."

Professor Figaro smiled and said nothing. The hock card. He shuffled and installed the deck back in the casebox and turned over the soda. A seven of clubs. He adjusted the cases. Ace of hearts lost and eight of clubs won. He thought of shutting down the faro and switching to poker or monte. Plummer coppered all his bets. They wanted his winnings. But more than that, they wanted his silence. If they could hold his money, they could be assured of his silence. They would not recruit him, but they would make sure he was either an ally or a corpse.

"This is a dangerous place, professor. My deputies and I keep a lid on it, keep the toughs at bay, but still a man takes his life in his hands going for a stroll here in this new camp, I'm told. I'd hate to have a worthy citizen waylaid in the night."

Randolph Figaro smiled and dealt. He had, in fact, removed most of his winnings from the back room at Churchill's and deposited them with the new mercantile, Stuart and Dance. And whenever he did, the bootblack in there, the sallow one known as Clubfoot George, solemnly stared.

"Now of course," Plummer continued, "you've got dust at Stuart and Dance's, a lot of it I imagine. But that's not healthy, you know. Unfriendly, we'd say. We've talked with Churchill here, and we're going into the banking business, professor. Tomorrow you'll withdraw what you have in Stuart and·Dance's safe and deposit it with the Bunton and Churchill Bank. That will assure these gents of your undying friendship and loyalty. These innocents sometimes say things that might be misunderstood by some outsider."

Professor Figaro smiled and leaned forward slightly, making his gray swallowtail coat gap at the breast and expose a shoulder-holstered revolver.

"I will think about it," said the gambler.

"Ah, but there's no time for that," said Henry Plummer. "No time at all."

Two competing stagecoach lines ran frequent coaches from Virginia and Bannack Cities to Salt Lake City, some four hundred miles away. These, plus the ox-drawn freight wagons plying the long trail, were the only practical way to get in and out of the Bitterroot Diggings. An obscure trail ran to Deer Lodge and on to Fort Benton, but it was little used, and indeed no steamer made it to Fort Benton in 1863.

Aristotle Scrimshaw idled casually about the wagon yard of the Peabody and Caldwell coach line. The morning stage had long since pulled out, with three men aboard—two drummers and a busted placer miner going east. Aristotle doubted that this coach would be robbed. The road agents always knew which coaches carried wealth, no doubt because of confederates operating as company employees. Then, too, other confederates at the various stops en route—especially at Dempsey's Ranch, and Bunton's Rattlesnake Ranch—duly noted what and who were aboard, and somehow made known to the road agents what coaches were worth the plucking. Some chalked sign would do it, Aristotle thought.

The yard was butchered into corrals, with a shed at one end for harness, hay piles, and miscellaneous gear under tarpaulins. A rude log shack sufficed as the stage office, waiting room, and dining parlor. No one lingered there now, hours away from any arrival or departure. Aristotle peered sharply and saw no one in the pale wintery sunlight. The object of his survey was a battered coach in the far corner of the yard, behind the corrals. It had not been used since it overturned at a mudslide in June, smashing the off side into a tangle of splintered maroon-lacquered wood and gilt open to the elements. Mud clung to the water-stained leather thoroughbrace that supported the coach body. Some wheel spokes had been shattered, too, a hound splintered, and the tongue and off-side singletree broken. Now it hulked useless, waiting to be cannibalized when the need arose.

Aristotle circled the coach thoughtfully, his keen mechanic's eye noting damage and soundness. Axles fine; hubs fine. Two off rear wheel spokes and one felloe shattered. Whole side of the coach itself caved in. Front seat missing; rear seat in place but ruined. Rear boot in place. Roof running rails in place. Tongue shattered . . . singletree broken but easily replaced. The wood and strap iron hound would be harder. . . .

It would have to be night work. He slipped out a measuring tape and took the dimensions of the tongue, length and girth. He'd make one. Singletrees were lying about and he'd borrow one. The hound he might splice. The shattered coach side he'd clean up and replace with canvas pulled taut. The missing seat he'd ignore—good for storage anyway. Oh, yes, the mud-soaked thoroughbrace seemed tight. . . .

The off rear wheel would be the hardest. He peered sharply about and still saw no one. He had no jack, but a lever would do. He'd prop up the axle and pull the wheel, and then what? Roll a stagecoach wheel as high as his chest down the gulch to his cabin? No. Two spokes cracked and a felloe broken. No, that wheel would have to stay right there. He studied it and knew exactly what he'd do. He'd make some collars of wet rawhide to fit around the cracked spokes, and these would dry into a solid splint. And he'd screw the broken felloe together with two small iron plates any blacksmith could make in ten minutes.

In thc harness shed he found the blackened old harness he hoped to find, piles of it. In one corner lay a heap, obviously thrown there for mending. It interested him. He'd prefer to borrow that than any harness in regular use. If he borrowed the coach from Peabody and Caldwell, he'd just as soon do no damage, and maybe even leave things better than he found them.

From the equipment standpoint, it all looked feasible, he thought. A coach that would last the four hundred miles, and enough harness. Still, he'd have to have horses. Not just the leaders and wheelers here, but replacements along the way, Peabody and Caldwell horses, Oliver coach company horses, or spares. There were no other harness horses in this raw camp; no question of buying any. No question either of negotiating with either Oliver or Peabody and Caldwell for the use of a few span. Their companies were shot through and through with spies and lackeys of the road agents. Aristotle thought to borrow the horses anyway, leave them at Salt Lake along with a payment for their use. Honest after a fashion, if not exactly what the owners might approve of.

He saw no other way. He had over four hundred pounds of gold to transport, plus his personal gear. He might indeed find some packhorses and packsaddles and all the rest somewhere in the camps, but the purchases would not go unnoticed and the agents would be ready. He might travel with the teamsters and their ox-drawn wagons, plodding on down through Idaho Territory and into Mormon country. But they, too, were watched and infested with spies, and not a bull train from the diggings that carried much wealth escaped attack. And often as not, several burly teamsters were murdered. He might try, too, with a large party of well-armed men. Some gold had gotten out that way, but more often than not, several within those parties turned out to be confederates of the agents, who got the drop on the others at the appropriate moment. No. . . .

A coach. A night coach, rolling through the vast concealing dark, with precious gold in its belly, while road agents slept because they knew of no traffic—that was the vision animating Aristotle Scrimshaw. There yet remained several large problems, though, most notably his traveling companions, because the task would be too large for a man alone. Whom could he trust? When he thought about it, the answer seemed plain enough: he could trust most anyone who also had a fortune to remove from the diggings. If a man had little or nothing, he would likely be a spy. If a man had a lot, and would prove it to Aristotle, then such a one might be trusted.

He needed four good men. Four men skilled with arms, not afraid of flying lead, able with horses, muscular enough to lift enormously heavy cases—and willing to risk their lives. A driver and shotgun messenger above; two armed riflemen, and gold, inside. And, given the weight of the gold, nothing else.

The road agents would follow, of course. A prize so large would lure them clear to the Overland Trail, if that is what it took to rob the night coach. Ideally, given the weight of the gold, he should have three span instead of two. But where would he find the harness horses? And the harness?

He slipped again into the harness shed and quietly began sorting out tugs and hames, collars and bellybands and breeching. In the repair pile lay enough harness for three span, but it would take fixing, a lot of fixing. He spotted someone in the log office now. A sulfur match flared and a wick caught and glowed. Aristotle slipped into the dusk and paused, watching and listening, and then hiked up the hill to the business district, where yellow lamps pierced the lavender November cold. He faced other problems, he thought: getting four hundred pounds of gold out of Stuart and Dance's unobserved, and down the steep hill to the night coach. That would be impossible, and he knew it. Someone, some regular in that mercantile, reported every transaction to the road agents. To withdraw a poke of gold from the green safe was to mark oneself for the grave. Maybe if he talked with Dance himself, got Dance to open up at night . . . maybe that would be the way. Dance seemed honest enough. Aristotle wandered down the aisles, peering in particular at carriage hardware, pricing canvas, pricing the smooth leather harness hanging from one rough-sawn whitewashed wall. And as he walked, he grew conscious of the stare of the lounging big bootblack, Clubfoot George Lane, whose gaze slid elsewhere whenever Aristotle glanced at him.

Chapter Three

The horses in the corrals were all facing one direction, their ears pricked forward. Beyond the corrals lay the long log shack for harness and gear, hulking black and shadowed under the half-moon. Frost silvered the hay piles, making them glow in the cold night. From behind the log shed came muffled thumps on the hard night air, perhaps the noises of theft.

Fortitude Hayes eyed the horses narrowly, watching their broad silver-splashed backs and necks and reading their alert postures and forward-cupped ears. Some dad-blasted highwayman or crook or drunken scum, he thought. He slid the twelve-gauge double-barreled sawed-off scattergun from its pegs on the wall of the Peabody and Caldwell station. He'd nail that varmint, he thought. Silently he slid the door closed behind him and oriented himself to the vaulting night, bright-coined by the icy moon.

One of the varmints was behind the shed, for sure. In the night air, the tap of a mallet reached him clearly. Where were the others? Gold-camp crooks usually operated in pairs; one a lookout, the other the one who stole the goods. Probably after harness or horseshoes—anything that could be bartered for food or a toss of the dice or the lay of a card.

He wasn't afraid. Fortitude Hayes had been plenty afraid in his time, but not now. For twenty years he'd been in the blue ranks of Uncle Sam's army, most of that time as a top sergeant. Then came Manassas and a minié ball in his hip, and a wound that wouldn't heal in the stinking Union field hospital. That's when he learned fear, in that filthy hospital surrounded by putrefying flesh; not when he formed up the ragged blue line, pounding bravery into green troops with his massive fists. The butchers had dug out the minié ball with their gore-caked instruments, and that had been the end of it. He even had to beg for water. He knew he'd mortify and cash in unless he did something, so he bribed an orderly and the orderly brought a pint of rotgut rye, and Fortitude poured the burning stuff into the hole and did it again day by day and never put his lips to the bottle. Somehow, he survived.

They cashiered him, gave him a blue-ribboned medal and let him keep his U.S.-issue revolver, and he limped his way west, the detritus of war, still a warrior, still able to commit mayhem with cold-blooded fury, but almost unable to walk. Still, a useful man in any stagecoach operation, and a man to deal out hell when dealing needed doing. He cracked the Colt Army and checked the loads and snapped it shut quietly. He limped into the corrals, his sharp eyes, peering from a mass of crow-footed and weathered flesh, finding nothing. No lookout. The horses stirred at his coming, but their attention was riveted on the noises from beyond the shed.

Fortitude slid between corral rails on the far side and eased into the shadow of the shed. The pounding grew clearer now on the heavy air. He'd nail that scum. His left pin was weak, but his sergeant-sized ham fists were as strong as ever, and if he didn't fill the crook with double-aught shot, he'd pulverize him. Or both. And without warning. That was how he did it on the road, up on the seat of the coaches. Whenever he saw the road agents sliding out ahead, getting set to stop and rob the coach, he started firing and kept on firing as fast as he could load the pair of shotguns with their paper cartridges, and that is how he had fended off three attempts now, by blasting the hell out of anything that moved. Word of that got around in Virginia City and made him a hero. And also a marked man. He got messages almost daily now, one way or another, telling him he was a dead man. But they only made him mad.

He peered around the north end of the long shed, finding nothing. There wasn't a lookout in sight, so he edged through its shadow until he could peer around the rear, or east, side, and there he found his man. The crook was hammering at the tongue of the old wreck of a coach back there. Fortitude took his time. He'd just wait and watch, and maybe catch two or three toughs instead of one, and maybe just haul their carcasses out to the growing Boot Hill over on the other side of the gulch.

This one looked lithe and muscular, sandy-haired and vaguely familiar. The fellow had knocked the broken tongue loose from its iron fittings and had put a new one in. In the bright moonlight, the tongue gleamed white. Now the crook was tapping the big bolts through holes augered in the tongue, and twisting the heavy nuts back on. It puzzled Fortitude. The crook paused to peer around—he seemed unarmed but Fortitude didn't doubt that there'd be a sidearm, at least, on the ground nearby. Next the crook removed the shattered singletree from a doubletree on the ground, replaced it with a sound one, and then bolted the doubletree onto the new tongue. This buzzard was obviously repairing this wreck of a coach. That idea set Fortitude to peering closer at the coach itself, rather than just the lowlife who tampered with it.

Now that he studied it, there were things to see. On the cracked spokes of the big off rear wheel were splintlike rawhide bandages that would be serviceable at least for a while. And—now that he examined it—the whole splintered mass of the coach body had been carefully sawed away, leaving the off side of the coach without any cowling. The white moonlight picked up more signs of industry—small iron plates bolted to a cracked felloe, driver's bench repaired and anchored where it had pulled off. The axles were blocked up, too, and Fortitude spotted a tar bucket and brush and knew the wheels had been greased and were turning freely now, even after months of neglect. So, he thought, enraged, this lowlife was going to nip a whole coach!

That was all the evidence he needed. He caromed around the shed and hissed words that sounded like gunshots.

"Up with the paws, you son of a bitch."

The sandy-haired man leapt, startled, and slowly lifted powerful mechanic's or miner's arms upward.

"Caught you stealing the coach," Fortitude snarled. "Your kind ends up on the hill up yonder. You're one of 'em, one of the road agents, only this time your sticky fingers done you in."

Aristotle stared uneasily at the terrible black bores of the shotgun.

"No," he said. "Not one of the agents. I was fixing to borrow this and maybe get free—"

"Borrow, ha! Peabody and Caldwell'd never see this wreck again."

"Borrow it," said Aristotle firmly. "I must get back to the states at once. Before consumption takes my son and the bank takes my farm. Get back with my diggings before the first of the year."

"Likely yarn," snarled Fortitude.

"You're Hayes," Aristotle said. "There's no man I'd rather see right now. You're the one man in the camp I'd trust. The one man who fights the road agents."

"Sing me your song, you bum, and then I'll plant you good," snapped Hayes.

Aristotle sighed shakily. "Like to lower my arms and talk. I'm unarmed."

"Where's your accomplice?"

"I'm alone. Name's Scrimshaw, and I've had some luck here, staked out a rich bar and picked up other claims. I've a tidy sum of dust up in Stuart and Dance's safe. Too much for packhorses. Needed a wagon, a coach, wheels. Thought I'd get this wreck shaped up, hire some help—I was planning to contact you since you're the one I trust most—and maybe get some other passengers who aren't afraid to shoot, and make a midnight run down to Fort Hall. And as for theft, no. Charge myself the regular ticket price, and the others, too, and add a bonus for using up horses and leave it with the company. Can't arrange it beforehand, for obvious reasons. The company'd have a workable coach again out of this."

Fortitude found himself liking the ring of that. He knew who Scrimshaw was; everyone knew. Scrimshaw was supposed to have taken more dust out than anyone else in Alder Gulch.

"Why should I believe that malarkey?" he growled.

"Take me to Dance and let him identify me."

"It's after midnight."

"Follow me to my cabin, then. Got a tintype of my wife, Annette, and me."

Fortitude sighed. He already knew that Scrimshaw was the man he said he was, and was telling the truth about borrowing—and paying for—the busted-up coach.

He lowered the shotgun. "Tell me the rest," he said. "And quiet-like, over here in shadow."

They hunkered down with their backs to the rough log wall of the shed.

"I got the wreckage cleaned away from the busted-up side, and I'm making a canvas piece, even with grommets, to tie in there, keep weather out and trigger fingers warm. Biggest problem now is horses. No draft horses available, so I thought to borrow and leave some dust. Other biggest problem is finding ones to trust. I figured I'd need four. You as shotgun messenger, a good driver—both from the company, so this has some . . . realism at the stage stops. Somehow I've got to get four hundred pounds of dust down here from Stuart and Dance's. Somehow I've got to find one or two others who want to try a run for it; get out. I don't know who, but they'd better have a strong reason or I won't trust them. Even at that, I don't plan to tell them when this night coach pulls out until the last moment. I'd just tell them to be ready every moment for the next forty-eight hours. Something like that anyway."

Fortitude whistled. "Four hundred pounds! The others'll have some, too. You get overloaded much and you'll need three span, not two."

Aristotle nodded. "I'd like to hire you, Hayes," he said. "And ask you to find a driver. Hire him, too. And deposit the ticket price with you before we go, just so you know that Peabody and Caldwell are picking up some business from it."

Fortitude was getting downright tickled with the whole prospect. "It'd serve them sons of bitches right if you got through. They've been watching for you, waiting for you. Whole camp knows it."

"They jumped me a few days ago. Got the letter from my wife, and they know I'm pulling out fast. They know that much. Will you help, Hayes?"

Fortitude smiled. "Reckon I might. As a matter of fact, a certain gent waylaid me just yestiddy about getting out. Fears for his life. He set up as a faro dealer down to Churchill's, not knowing who the crowd in there would be, and now he's trapped. Name's Figaro, Professor Randolph Figaro."

Aristotle frowned. "Last person I want is some tinhorn gambler with ties to the Churchill saloon. I'd say no to him."

"You ain't thinkin', son," said Fortitude. "First, he's as good with a short gun as anyone in these parts. Second, he's got ears; he hears a bunch. When they spill their plans, he hears it all. He hears who they're gonna jump and when; he hears about robberies after they happened. He'd hear anything they pick up about you, and this."

"But he's one of them."

"Under sentence of death, boy. He's been ordered to pull his winnings out of Dance's and turn it over to them as a surety, as a bond for silence. Only once they get his dust they'll do him in, sure as shooting. So he hasn't pulled out his dust, and he's looking hard for an exit pass outa here. I'd get him on board anytime."

Aristotle thought. "Anyone else?" he asked at last.

"Sure, people come to me all the time, whisper stuff, how can I get out? and all that. Nothing I could do until now. I allus told 'em no, cain't do anything. This place and every coach stop for miles is full of spies and agents. Bunton's Rattlesnake Ranch is the worst. Same's true on the Oliver line. We each got our own horses, but we use the same stops. Sure, I got people asking. They figure they can whisper to me, at least, and they're right. I got one. . . ."

He wondered if he should even open the subject. Scrimshaw would be shocked out of his socks. But what the devil. . . .

"A madam over to Bannack City is aching to pull out with her earnings. Her man, Alfonso, who's some tiger in a brawl, comes up to me and asks how to do it. She's got a lot of dust to haul."

"No women!" cried Aristotle. "We're likely to get shot at. There won't even be a front seat in this coach. I want fighters, good strong men, not some old—whore!"

"All right, then, forget her. Only she's the shootingest Mex lady every held a short gun in her little hands."

"I won't haul ill-gotten gold in this coach."

"Don't know as it's so ill-gotten, lad. Two, three thousand men in these camps and almost no respectable women, and all of them getting the ache now and then."

In truth, Fortitude was himself a steady customer of Angelica Ramirez and her girls, and liked the dignified Mexican madam.

"I'll think about it," said Scrimshaw shortly. "Meanwhile, get more information. How much dust, how many pounds. And whether she's bringing this Alfonso, the one that can fight. And don't say a damned thing about these plans."

"Reckon I'll just do that," Fortitude said. "You got this coach ready, or do you want more help? By the way, that new tongue, shiny white wood, is a giveaway."

Fortitude fetched a pail of water from the gulch and soon enough the new wood and repairs of the coach were covered with a dark film of gumbo mud, and the wounded carriage looked as forlorn as ever.

"I'll go over it by daylight tomorrah," Fortitude said. "I reckon I can be limping around here without arousing the furies.

Maybe I'll see something you missed in the dark. You gonna take that tar bucket with you?"

"Leave it beside the shed," Aristotle said. "It looks like another piece of coach-yard equipment."

"What'd you have in mind for harness?"

"That'll be next. I'm going to mend that pile in there, pull it together with baling wire if I have to. Fix that and not disturb the good stuff hanging from the pegs."

Fortitude nodded. "Maybe I can fiddle with some myself. You know, Scrimshaw, you're crazy as a loon. Only a crazy turkey would try this. They got ears. They'll jump this outfit and your four hundred pounds of dust five miles down the gulch from here. But"—he grinned—"I'm crazy, too. I'm going to have a leetle powwow with Cal Creed. He's a square shooter and driver and was with me them times we got jumped. He just put the heat to the cayuses, a-howling like a banshee. He got nipped by flyin' lead here a bit ago, caught some shoulder flesh, but that was three weeks back and I guess he's a-raring for revenge. I got you a catamount of a driver who bites bullets and spits 'em back."

"I can't imagine a better man," said Aristotle. "I'd like to offer you each a hundred in dust—in advance. Do you think that'd make your wage?"

Shotgun messenger wages for two months, Fortitude thought. And two months of driver wages, too. "It's generous," he said. "Likely I'd of done this for the sheer hell of it—maybe nail some hides to the wall."

Scrimshaw gathered up his tools. "Done for tonight," he said. "I'll be back tomorrow to try on the canvas I've been cobbling up, and start on the harness. Meet me here and tell me about Creed and the rest."

They shook on it and Fortitude watched the compact miner slip into the night. A brave one, the former sergeant thought, and brave ones usually got killed. For a moment he pined for two good legs and one good squad of seasoned boys in blue. Let his army loose and he'd clean out these road agents and hounds of hell in a week, string them up or send them packing with the fear of God in them.

He had a run scheduled in the morning, and he suddenly realized he wouldn't be here tomorrow night. He would take the coach as far as Fort Hall, lay over, and bring one up here the following day. Well, Scrimshaw'd figure it out. But it sure as hell would delay the night run four or five days. And he'd have to get Creed lined out, too. Creed hadn't driven for a while because of that wound, but he'd be ready. Trouble was, Creed liked to blab. Best driver around, and hell on wheels when agents tried to halt a coach. The only man Fortitude had ever seen scramble out on the back of a trotting wheel horse and cut a dead lead horse, shot by bandits, out of the harness and keep right on a-going, all the while dodging bullets. That was some going.

Creed would be up in the rooming house on the high end of Wallace. The place had ears. That'd have to wait until morning. He'd have to get over to Bannack, too, for a talk with Angelica Ramirez. She'd likely have so much dust it'd take a freight wagon. And would she take the girls and all the rest? He'd find that out soon enough.

This fool's coach would likely need three span of horses, carrying all that dust. That'd upset the whole Caldwell and Peabody operation. He grinned. Company'd come out of it all right, cash in the till, fixed-up coach.

As he walked through the silvery night toward the solid little log cabin he had down-gulch from the company yards, he sensed a presence behind him. He didn't turn, though he itched to glance at the stalker from the corner of his eye. His heart speeded. He loved the game. It sent a charge of wild tumult through his tough body. A commonplace thing. Anyone out of his nest in the middle of the night in these camps took his life and purse in hand.

He saw shade ahead, a rocky bluff that produced a narrow moon shadow at its base. But it lay too far off. The faint crush of footsteps on gravel came hard now, a sudden patter. He whirled, wishing he had kept the scattergun rather than returning it to its pegs, and the hooligan was on him.

"Up with your hands, you son of a bitch. Up or you die!" rasped a muffled voice.

Fortitude Hayes roared, swung, and closed as a revolver shot shredded the peace. The ball seared his left armpit and stung him. Fortitude snarled and landed a huge fist in the hooligan's gut, expelling a gust of rancid air and sending the revolver clattering. Fortitude's right boot landed on a shin, and he heard a hoarse yelp. Then the hooligan fled, scrambling into the blackness, while Fortitude hastened him along with two shots from the revolver. On the third pull of the trigger it misfired.

Had the hooligan witnessed the whole thing with Scrimshaw? If so, the miner's night run would be doomed.

Chapter Four

Below them, at the bottom of an endless grade, glowed the lamplights of Bannack City, soft and smudged in the black November night. The dark Concord coach under Fortitude swayed on its leather braces as Gil Train, sitting next to him, let the coach press into the breeching of the wheel team, hurrying the horses the last mile.

"Looks like we made it without getting jumped—so far," Fortitude muttered. "Must have thin-purse drummers down there."

The two porky salesmen in the dark coach probably heard him, but he didn't care. For whatever reason, the road agents hadn't bothered to stop them this time.

He disliked these fall and winter runs, not because it had grown cold—the buffalo robe around him usually took care of that—but because so much of the run from Virginia City to Bannack City had to be done in darkness. He always figured the road agents had the advantage of him at night. He couldn't see much, except when the moon glinted full, but they could usually see him and the driver silhouetted against the starlit skies. By day he started shooting the instant he spotted a robbery in the making—a glint of sun on a barrel, horses closing from one side or another, log barriers across the rutted road. But at night he had to wait for the sons of bitches to shoot and then reply to the muzzle flash, making a flash of his own.

Gil Train, beside him, seemed a good enough driver, but not fierce like Cal Creed, not ready to whoop up the team at the smallest sign of trouble. Train didn't really believe that he might be safer speeding than standing. Fortitude muttered under his breath, cussing the night, while Train threaded into Bannack, rumbling along a wide dirt street and across Grasshopper Creek. He had a good hand, and pulled up the coach before the lamplit Peabody and Caldwell offices without touching the brakes.

"Layover," he yelled to the drummers inside. "Fetch yourself a meal and a bunk. Hash house across the bridge; couple, three hotels around."

Fortitude peered down from his seat while Train jumped down into some horse apples on the road. Nine-fifteen; right on schedule, he thought. Sheriff Plummer stood to one side, smiling affably, his eyes studying each drummer thoughtfully. He always did that, Fortitude thought; met every stagecoach. The sheriff had an exact idea of who came to Bannack City, who went to Virginia City, who seemed to be leaving either place.

"Evenin', Sheriff," said Fortitude. "Looking for someone?"

"Ah, Mr. Hayes. I see you made it. No road agent trouble?"

"You'd have heard of it by now," retorted Fortitude. "Let a miner leave the country with a poke and you'd hear of it soon enough."

"They're terrible, those agents," Plummer said.

Fortitude thought to tell the blasted sheriff to do something about it, but bit his tongue. There'd been whispers about Plummer himself. The man lived awfully high on a sheriff salary. Bought a lot on Second Cross Street and was building a fine house. Smoked fat cigars, got himself married to a handsome woman from Sun River, entertained every notable in the country.

Fortitude glared at the night-shrouded town. The surrounding foothills vaulted blackly up to some vague horizon where stars hung. Shank of the evening, he thought. First some vittles and then a private little visit to Angelica. . . .

"You bunking in the company yard tonight, Fortitude?" asked Plummer.

Fortitude grinned and winked. At last he lowered the shotgun in his hand, peeled away the robe, and clambered down. He almost collapsed when he hit the clay because his legs had gone stiff, so he stomped. Behind him he heard Train clamber up again and steer the horses and coach into the yard for the night. The company night hostler would unharness the two span. Fortitude peered around the quiet street. No one outside in the chill, but every saloon lit like Christmas. He felt Plummer's gaze on his back and didn't like it. He'd always figured that beneath Plummer's bland veneer lurked a man who'd shoot anyone in the back. The drummers, each toting two portmanteaus, had vanished.

Fortitude limped along, wondering whether business or chow came first. Private business. He decided on the business first and headed south until he hit the first cross street, and then west, out onto Yankee Flats. Nestled at a discreet distance from the rest of the gold town, a row of log buildings lay shrouded by night except for faint red glows of swinging breeze-tossed lanterns. He glanced back and thought he saw Plummer staring at him from a well-lit corner. But he didn't care. Let the sheriff think what he would: this leetle trip wasn't to benefit his loins, but other things, such as his pride and curiosity and, by God, his other itch, which was to blast a few road agents into the bottom layer of hell.

A gust of November chill heeled him as he opened the heavy rouged door and entered Angelica's place. A step farther and a wall of warmth smacked him, warmth from the nickel-trimmed black parlor stove in the front salon. Fancy joint. The front room could have been a church parlor except it shimmered the color of sin. Not a soul here. Only a pair of lamps burning in a single stand and empty orange silk seats. He heard a woman's high laughter from somewhere back in the bowels of the whorehouse. Must be someone in the bar, he thought, turning left and entering a solid small room with a mahogany bar and mirrored back bar. A mulatto girl, yellow as sunflowers, poured spirits behind the bar. She could be purchased. Anything here could be purchased—except Angelica. Many had tried it, just to see if the legend was true. She'd once been offered a thousand dollars in dust for one hour—a thousand an hour!—and had politely refused.

Fortitude peered around the saloon, studying two men—suit-coated, not miners—perched on stools there.

"Where's the madam?" asked Fortitude even before the yellow girl could offer him a drink.

"Hold your horses," the girl said. "And if you can't wait, I'll fix you up in an instant, sonny."

"What is it, Juana?" asked Angelica, materializing in the doorway. "Oh, it's you, Señor Hayes."

In the warm lamplight Angelica looked halfway pretty, Fortitude thought. Might have been a Latin beauty when she was young. But now she was heavier and always encased in thick, costly black, in some sort of perpetual mourning.

"Come into my office and we'll discuss the girls," she said softly, her liquid brown eyes gazing blankly at the two in checkered suit coats sipping at the bar.

Fortitude eyed the strangers himself. Good to remember mugs when in clandestine business, he thought. If he saw those faces hanging around again, he'd take them for road agents. He followed her quietly into her barren office and beyond, into the next chamber, her own quarters. She left the door open. He'd never been here, in a room with her own heavy carved bed, ornate armoires, whitewashed log walls, naked except for two tintypes of boys and a small crucifix.

"I always leave the door open," she said. "I wouldn't want anyone to have a wrong impression."

From their vantage point in the shaded room they could see across the business *sala,* and into the saloon.

"We will talk quietly," she said, her gaze weighing and alert. "Your man talked with me."

"Bueno."

"I think I have something for you."

She waited quietly, saying nothing, distrust in her coarse-fleshed ivory face.

"A coach," he said. "In a few nights."

"When and who, *por favor*?"

"I can't say, and can't name names."

She shrugged, dismissing him. "I must know," she said. "Would you care to stay for sport?"

"They're as worried about you as you are about them."

"That's not enough."

"They have a lot to take out. You have a lot to take out. Anyone who has a lot to get out can be trusted."

"I would have to see it with my own eyes."

"How much do you have—to get out?"

"I can't tell you. Let's say *nada,* nothing." She smiled blandly, her glance upon the open door.

He'd seen the monstrous black iron box beside her bed before. It had a pair of handles riveted to its sides. Silently he limped to it and gripped the handles. It didn't budge. Not even a violent jerk, his best effort, budged the iron lock box.

She watched, liquid-eyed.

Irritation oiled up in Fortitude. "Angelica, a coach can carry only so much. One of the others has a heavy load. An overload could exhaust the teams, wear them down, delay us, endanger the trip."

She shrugged. "*Verdad,* I don't know."

"All right, how much in dollars?"

"Much, much. Maybe I'll wait, not go."

"Maybe that's a good idea. The lighter the better."

"No, no, I was just joking. Time is running out. I feel it. I must go or lose it. They'll come, kill Alfonso just like that, and take it."

"The other party has four hundred pounds."

"*Dios!* I have more, I know that. Too much, maybe."

"We can't take it in this, Angelica. I want it put in containers, any kind strong enough, no more than a hundred pounds each so that one or two men can carry it. Saddlebags, maybe."

"I think maybe six hundred pounds," she said softly.

He stared. Six hundred. And four hundred. And passengers. Over half a ton of gold. That meant three span for sure, and maybe Figaro and Scrimshaw ought to ride horses beside the coach, too. Slow, too slow.

"I'll get word to you."

"I must know the others. And know when."

"You'll have to take almost nothing—of this. One bag, Angelica. You'll have to be ready anytime. Ready to pick up your bag and walk out, just like that."

"Bueno."

"And I can't give you names yet."

"Why should I trust anyone? Even you."

Fortitude felt hot. "I don't care whether you get out with your loot or not," he snarled, too loud. He felt sorry at once. Those who idled in the smoke-hazed bar two doors away either didn't hear or pretended not to.

Her eyes rebuked him. She smiled suddenly, her lightly carmined lips spreading. "Sport, señor?"

"Food," he replied.

"Come back afterward. I'll have—

"I'll send word," he said. "Word from the virgin."

"The virgin?"

"You'll hear from the virgin," he said, leering faintly. "Be ready anytime. Anytime."

"Madre de Dios," she said.

He rode shotgun messenger down to the Adobes at Fort Hall on the Oregon Trail, the station for Peabody and Caldwell as well as Ben Holladay's Overland, Gil Train driving the whole way. Three passengers, one a miner, but no trouble. The miner looked busted. Along the road they exchanged news with teamsters. No trouble. They laid over and brought the coach back, this time with four pilgrims, one of them a sloppy new high-yellow girl for one of Bannack City's fancy houses.

Before they started, Fortitude got into an argument with Train.

"We got to take a spare span back to Virginia," he said. "They're needing it."

"Where'd you hear that?"

"They need it. Harness up."

"Not my job," the driver snarled. "Git the hostlers to do it. Whole thing sounds like some mix-up."

Fortitude lumbered into the station office and collared a hostler, a skinny lunkhead kid. "One more span, and bust your butt," he bristled, sergeant-talking. Sergeants all knew how to talk when talking was needful. The kid heard the clash and growl and snarl of it, and hustled out muttering. A third span got harnessed and hitched, leaders. Fortitude handed the long lines to Train, who cursed them and snagged them into paws already full of lines.

Then they left. Fortitude fought the battle at every station, bullying the hostlers into harnessing a third span and trading in the used-up horses. They rattled into Bannack City in the morning of a cold, overcast day, but Sheriff Plummer idled there as usual to meet them, his intelligent eyes noting at once the third span.

"You carrying weight, Train?"

"Nah, just pilgrims. They want the goddamn horses at V.C. Pain in the butt."

They unloaded two pilgrims and the woman at Bannack and picked up three miners, all prosperously dressed in new storeboughts. Off to the Alder Gulch digs, they announced too loudly.

Henry Plummer smiled. "Have a safe trip, boys," he said, leaning on the maroon varnish of the coach just under Fortitude.

From his seat above, the shotgun messenger could see a hideout gun shoulder-holstered under Plummer's expensive gray gentleman's suit. The sheriff stood straight. Gil Train snapped lines and snarled, and six horses lurched into a trot. Fortitude Hayes peered over the edge of his seat, down to the cowling of the coach. Where Plummer's hand had rested, he saw a smear.

"We're going to get it this time, Gil. When I say go, you git! We got six horses this time, not four. They could kill two and we'd still make it dragging the stiffs."

"Prefer not to do that. Get ourselves mortified doing it," Train muttered as the team walked up the long, soft grade out of Bannack and broke over a barren, sage-dotted ridge.

Fortitude snarled, then shut up. Train would get him killed even before Scrimshaw's night run. Hauling out a half ton of gold fascinated him. If he was going to get himself shot, he hoped it'd be playing jackpot poker. Not now. Then it came to him.

"Stop this outfit a minute, Gil."

"What for?"

"Stop it a minute," Fortitude yelled, turning sergeant again.

When the coach lurched to a stop, he clambered down and rubbed the smudge out.

"What was that all about?" Gil asked tartly.

"Dirt."

Train glared at him. Dumb miners stared out the window.

Twenty minutes later they slid into a cottonwood-lined meadow nestled in dry rock cliffs, and pulled up before a shabby log hut surrounded by spider legs of corral fence. Bunton's Rattlesnake Ranch, first station east of Bannack City.

"Grow rattlesnakes here," Fortitude growled. Two-legged ones, he figured. Of all the road agent places on this road, this dump was king.

"Five minutes, gents," Train yelled down.

The miners in their store-boughts clambered down, making the leather thoroughbraces groan and creak, and pissed beer on sagebrush, not bothering to see if a woman might be in the cabin. The remaining preacherish pilgrim stayed in the coach.

"Get a third span harnessed, goddammit," Fortitude yelled.

"No need for it. Leave the nags here," replied a narrow-skulled moron hostler with two lethal but filthy revolvers dog-earing from his waist.

"They have call for the span in V.C.," said Fortitude patiently. He leaned over to the hostler. "Maybe they'll take a heavy load out tomorrah," he whispered confidentially.

"Yeah, maybe. I'd better get a span under leather," the man said, grinning. "I'll git some good ones."

Sure, Fortitude thought. Good ones. Which would be traded at the next stop, Dempsey's Ranch. Another gem of a place. He spat, and his juice curled into a dust ball on the clay.

A bunch of hardcases gawked and joked, and made bawdy talk with the dumb miners in store-boughts.

Seven minutes later, when the coach rattled out, swaying on its braces and lurching over a potholed portion of road, Fortitude peered once again over the side of his seat and saw once again a smear of mud on the varnish.

He cussed. Two horsemen passed, going in the direction of the coach but not looking at it. Fortitude followed them with the bores of his scattergun, cussing. Let one just slow his nag, and he'd be digesting double-aught shot. But the riders looked smarter than that and hustled on, and Fortitude cussed and memorized mugs again. He had a pretty good mug collection in his skull, his own private rogues' gallery.

"Thought they might be agents," Gil muttered.

"They were agents. No-goods from Bunton's sending word up the line that we got three fat Hibernians."

"Got six horses and a light load. Maybe I'll run," Gil muttered.

"If you don't run, I'll unload this scattergun in your crotch, Train."

They'd pay this time, he thought. Midafternoon. Cold and sunny, kind of magnifying air that showed him every blade of grass. See-through air. See-around air. He peered under his robe where the second double-barreled scattergun lay blue on the floorboards. He hoisted his holster around and clamped a paw around the grip of his Army. Like war, he thought. Cavalry. He'd been infantry.

They hit the Beaverhead River and forded it, wallowing through water that washed between wheel spokes. The river ran sullenly between featureless sagebrush flats. They turned north on the far bank and ran the ruts toward Dempsey's up a piece past Beaverhead Rock. Pretty safe place, Fortitude thought. River on one side, empty flats that couldn't hide an Injun on the other. Some stinking black mountains far off to the east.

But from a crease he'd forgotten about, horses boiled out of nowhere, a dozen of them, each ridden by a gent in a low sombrero, wearing a yellow rag with two holes stabbed in it for eyes. Fortitude leveled the scattergun.

"Start running, Gil," he roared.

Chapter Five

Standing in a foot of icy water, Aristotle Scrimshaw shoveled gravel into a tin bucket and hauled the bucket to his slab-wood sluice box on the creek bank. The bar he worked, above Virginia City and just below Bill Fairweather's discovery claim, still ran so rich he could see glints of gold in the coarse sands. He dumped the gravel and river muck over the upper end, and followed with a bucket of water, letting it all churn over the riffles, or cleats, that would trap the heavy gold but permit the lighter gravel to wash past.

He rocked the box a little, automatically, his mind elsewhere. He'd performed this ritual so often over the past months that he no longer considered what he was doing, but studied the alder thickets that jammed the narrow gulch. This frost-sharp morning he wrestled with a new set of demons: how to escape from here alive and with the fruits of his grueling labor. Fortitude Hayes had vanished the day before. Off to Fort Hall, the Peabody agent had told him. Back in three days.

Three more days of delay, while his family suffered. His son lay dying. The bank would foreclose in the middle of winter. He slopped another pail of water into the box and wrestled with his dilemma, but no answers came. He didn't know how to get his pokes down to the coach yard without discovery. They watched him. Probably someone peering right that moment from some thicket in this rough-rock-and-shrub gulch. That wasn't the end of it, either. He had eleven good claims to sell somehow. That or abandon them. They'd be jumped the instant he left the district. But selling them would be a flag, a public announcement. . . .

Someone labored on foot up the gulch, and Aristotle edged closer to his new revolver, another Navy, lying on the grass beside the sluice box. A big man, in work blues, by the looks of him. Aristotle glanced covertly, and scraped yellow dust and half a dozen pea-sized nuggets off the wood behind the riffles, and funneled the gold into the new poke, his thirty-fourth. The big one labored straight toward him. A visitor, then. Vaguely familiar, but not someone he knew well.

Aristotle stopped work and slid the holster closer, easing the blue Navy from it.

"You're Scrimshaw," the man called from twenty yards. He seemed out of breath.

Aristotle nodded. The man labored up the last few yards, and then Aristotle put a name to the face and holstered his Navy. Before him stood a thick giant, well over six feet, with a smooth vast nose hooked like an eagle's beak, dividing a pair of small gray arrogant eyes.

"You're Cal Creed," said Aristotle. Fortitude told him that Creed had a skull thick enough to stop a bullet, and a conceit to match it. A good enough description, Aristotle thought, resting on his shovel.

"Good. I was hoping you'd know me. That's a tough walk and I'm still poorly."

"Wound healed up?"

"Getting there. I can work now, though a day or two more would help." He paused, staring coldly. "Hayes hauled me out of my bunk before he left, yanked me into an ice-cold street, walked me out of earshot of everyone, told me you need a driver soon, and bought me flapjacks as an apology."

Aristotle grinned. "Sounds like the sergeant."

"You want to tell me about it?"

"A little."

"I need it all before I make up my mind."

"I think your mind was made up before you came here," Aristotle rejoined. "Or you wouldn't have come."

Creed glared. He didn't like smart talk, obviously.

Aristotle glanced sharply at the autumn-bare thickets, and then began quietly. He had to get back to his family fast and with gold. The coach repair. His heavy load. The night run. Three span if possible. The others . . . Aristotle hesitated. That gambler, Figaro, and a—a madam at Bannack, someone called Angelica, with a heavy load. A hundred in dust to drive the coach south, plus fare.

"Pay, hell," Creed retorted. "Doc dug their lead outa me; now I'll get my revenge."

"Revenge?"

"Getting your gold out. Blasting lead into them if I get the chance."

"I hope you don't get the chance," Aristotle replied. "I hope the run's such a surprise they never get organized."

"I'd prefer to blast the hell out of them," Creed retorted.

No arguing with a human bull, Aristotle concluded. "The coach is ready. Have a look if you want, but don't be obvious. I'm still working on harness, but maybe tonight I'll have it cobbled up."

"Since I'm driving, I get to choose the night. Need enough light to see."

"Moon's coming on full soon."

Creed nodded. "How are you going to get your gold out of Dance's safe?"

Aristotle pulled a work-hardened hand through his sandy hair. "Talk to Walter Dance, I suppose. I want him to let me in at night, when there's not a soul around. Especially Lane, the bootblack. He hovers around whenever Walter's writing receipts or handing pokes in or out."

Creed nodded. "Let me know when you're ready. I'm in."

With that, he started down the gulch, never looking back. Aristotle watched him go. Now another one knows, he thought.

He glanced up at the sun. High. Almost noon. About the time Walter Dance would leave the mercantile in the hands of his clerk and walk three blocks to his new cottage of rough-sawn board and sit down before a hot lunch ritually prepared by Mrs. Dance.

Aristotle patiently scraped the last of the coarse flakes and tiny nuggets from the riffles, and carried his tools to his tiny log cabin. He anchored the holstered Navy to his waist and started for Virginia City. Now'd be as good a time as ever to catch Dance, he thought. He hated toting the heavy sidearm, but in a world as violent and sudden as this one, he had no choice.

The noon sun had gone weak and powerless and niggardly with its warmth. Losing ground. Good working weather, though. Not like the breathless scorch of midsummer, when he found excuses to loll through the early afternoons. Annette needed him. Needed him yesterday, needed him months ago. He should have been less greedy. He trudged down the gulch, past other rawboned men clawing flaked gold from an obscure mountain gulch with vicious determination.

Oddly, he couldn't remember Annette. Her face refused to form in his mind; the images of his boy and girl refused to come to him, either. The farm came clearer: glacial grassy hills, hardwoods along the creek, hickory, box elder, lots of maples. Incredible black loam in the bottoms that curled shining off his plow as Jimbob strained in the worn harness. He needed somehow to think of Annette. He'd lived without desire here, suppressing the vagrant night thoughts of her that would torment him if he'd let them. He'd come to think of her as a friend, his confidante. But her face refused to form, and he'd have to study the tintype in his cabin to bring her alive in his soul again, and even then he'd not have her voice. Now she needed him, and his mind keened its answer to her, and he wished he could fling a message across the ether to her: *I'm coming. I'm coming now. Wait for me, hang on. . . .*

He crossed the rawboned, rutted street and entered Dance and Stuart's. A cowbell jangled. The place snaked thin back from Wallace Street, a heap of careless logs half cured, daubed with clay to fend off the weather. He felt his boots gouge the puncheon floor as he blindly bulled into the belly of the snake.

"Sir?" asked a clerk.

"Dance. Is he in?"

A voice rose from across the aisle. "Off to lunch, Scrimshaw. You got a poke to deposit?"

The long, grinning monkey George Lane had addressed him.

"Not this time," said Aristotle. He wheeled out, offers of messages in his ears.

He started up Jackson toward Dance's, paused, sensed Lane's eyes on him from the small cracked air-bubbled real-glass window, and decided to be less obvious. Five minutes later he knocked on Walter Dance's plank door, having lollygagged his way through town, up Van Buren, down Idaho, watching and being watched by rough, lounging men under rain-stained gray porch roofs.

Mrs. Dance opened. One of two or three virtuous women in Virginia City, and too plain to be otherwise.

"A word with Walter if I may, Mrs. Dance."

She nodded, white-jowled, and stepped aside for him.

The crude cottage, one of the first built in Virginia City, had only two rooms, one for living and eating, the other for sleeping. Walter Dance hunkered over a white vitreous bowl of stew. He peered up sourly, annoyed by interruption.

"What do you want, Scrimshaw?" he asked, wanting to get back to his spooning.

"You're busy. I'll catch you at a better time—"

"Now that you're here, get on with it."

"I'll be fetching my pokes from the safe shortly. I thought—"

"Well, come do it. I'll be there."

"There's a lot. I'd like to come with you at night, very late. Not with people around."

Dance peered up at him from bagged black eyes, licking stew from his black walrus mustache, fingering the white napkin he'd bibbed into his brown flannel shirt.

"Don't see the need of it," he said.

"I'm watched. They know—the road agents know—"

"I don't see the need of it. I've got business hours."

Aristotle paused. Dance had a merchant's mind: profit, loss, and inventory. Maybe he would understand history. "Every time a miner's taken his gold from your safe, he's disappeared. Collie Reich, Jim Bowen, Sherman Lansdale—they say scores."

Black furrows built over Dance's black eyes. "What happens outside of my store isn't my responsibility, Scrimshaw."

Aristotle didn't want to say what festered in his head, but he might hint. "Maybe what happens inside is connected with what happens outside."

Dance dabbed at juiced gray bloodless lips with the napkin. "Good as I can hire. Honest enough. Lane's a pretty industrious fellow, bad foot and all. When he's not blacking, he's shelving merchandise for me, fast as they freight it in. Wilburforce—honest enough, if I hear what you're saying. No. Business hours, Scrimshaw. I'll not skulk around at night and get knocked in the head for it."

"I'll pay you something to help me get it out after midnight—sometime soon."

"What you do is your business," said Dance patiently. The tone was dismissive.

Aristotle contained a bursting need to tell Dance to go to hades. That was how he talked, hades. Pulling thirty-four heavy pokes of gold out in broad daylight with Clubfoot George Lane and Wilburforce and God knew who else watching would be roughly the same as suicide, and Dance knew it.

"Suppose I slip you some dummies, pokes full of rock. And he next day I pick those up in broad daylight and get the real pokes after hours. Or before hours. How about before sunup, Walter?"

Dance belched, set his napkin down on the rough plank table impatiently, his siesta hour delayed.

"Young man, you get yourself an armed guard and come fetch your dust according to normal hours. Proper men live by proper hours. No room in that little safe for dummy pokes anyway. I'm thinking of getting out of that business. It's nothing but a headache: receipts, records, and now accusations. Henry Elling'll have his bank open in a few weeks anyway. Now if you'll excuse me—"

"I'll fetch it soon, Walter," Aristotle said, backing out. "Good day, and to you, Mrs. Dance."

Dance stared sulfurously as Aristotle slid the plank door shut.

Now two more knew, he thought. At least he could go for the gold at some moment when George Lane wasn't about. But the other one, Wilburforce, would probably blab. Even so, he might have an hour or two to cache it before the toughs found out. After that it'd be hades. No place to hide. No place to cache. Maybe half the men on the streets two-bit spies and blabbers for the road agents. It'd take two horses with heavy packsaddles and strong panniers to haul his thirty-four pokes. Not that they'd take up space—but they'd weigh so much. He'd better give some thought to that, to containers, to sturdy horse-loads. . . . Plan it all out and it might work, even in broad daylight. Maybe daylight would be his salvation. The road agents hated it, wore elaborate masks, even long blankets over their horses. Yes, thought Aristotle, daylight. Broad bright daylight.

He stood on Dance's porch, staring down at the sprawling new camp below him. Five months old and something like three hundred buildings, he'd heard. New ones finished each day, raw and ugly as the humped dry mountains here. Log and canvas, fieldstone and mud mortar. Roofs of poles and thick sod. Packing-box furniture and floors. Adzed beams, whipsawed plank, what little there was of it. Red-mudded Virginia City was nobody's vision of alpine glory.

He felt alone. Odd how a man felt alone here. Not like the hollowed glacial hills and knitted villages of southern Wisconsin, where people seemed neighbors and farm kitchens always burst with friends sucking coffee or something harder, leaning back two-legged on groaning chairs. Nothing like that in mining camps. Isolated men, distrustful and rightly so, with rough, murderous wolves dawdling on every front stoop.

He drifted toward the Oliver express office, source of all fast mail coming to the camp. Maybe a letter from Annette. He remembered her now, her patient gray eyes and wry, disbelieving smile. . . . A pessimist if ever there was one. But the good kind, the kind who struggled and endured no matter what, all the more courageous because she felt certain nothing would come out right. "Fly home, Aristotle," she'd written so long ago. Now he would. He'd hug her taut body. She'd always been taut when he hugged her, as if he shouldn't hug her and she shouldn't enjoy being hugged. She'd stand stiffly like a statue for painful moments, and then dissolve. Once the dissolving, the melting began, she turned mad with passion, the abandoned puritan. Desire flooded him and he let it linger for the first time in two years. He heard her soft, urgent voice across the vast continent, across eternal prairies, across deep swift rivers, across humped hills.

Oliver had worked some mining camp magic. In a city of log and canvas and dirt roofs, the company office of board and batt seemed almost permanent. Inside, solidly fitted golden oak counters and wickets spanned the back wall. Each of the wickets had a grilled window, and behind the barred windows were tough clerks in white shirts, suit coats, and cravats. Since June, Oliver & Company had expressed mail up from the Overland and California trails, a dollar apiece going or coming.

Nothing for Mr. Scrimshaw.

Aristotle bought a postcard. "I'm catching a stagecoach out in the next few days," he wrote boldly, using a company nib and company inkpot. That'd cost a buck, too. A good message for stray eyes to see, he thought, letting the clerk siphon a dollar of dust from his poke onto a brass balancing scale. They knew he was going anyway. They'd mugged him simply to get Annette's letter.

Saddlebags, he thought, laboring upslope to Pfouts and Russell, the other general mercantile in the camp.

"Paris," he said, "what have you in saddlebags?"

"Not a thing. I'm helpless, depending on Salt Lake freight. They send what they feel like," replied Paris Pfouts from behind his vast walrus. "You taking off, Scrim?"

Coming from any other man, the question would have aroused suspicion in Aristotle. Coming from Paris it could mean anything, including help. Pfouts had lost so much merchandise to the road agents he could scarcely work through a sentence without salting it with imprecations against forces of darkness.

"Soon," he replied quietly, his eyes surveying three other customers, all out of earshot.

"You have a way?"

"Maybe."

"You need something to carry with." It was a statement.

"Yes."

"For two horses, I'll wager. Town gossip—they keep track of you, Scrim—says twenty-eight pokes in Dance's."

Aristotle smiled politely.

"Two loads," said Pfouts, "and fifty loyal armed men." He laughed sardonically. "Especially loyal," he added.

Scrimshaw grinned.

"Haven't a saddlebag or pannier or packsaddle in here. But yonder on the counter is an entire tanned hide, right out of the empire of the Latter-day Saints. You handy with an awl and thong? Or rivets?"

"I'm handy," said Aristotle.

He felt the hide. Excellent tanning, strong and pliable, an even russet color.

"Fifty in dust."

"That's a lot."

"Dollar a pound just to ship it here. Nineteen pounds. I'll throw in some rivets I got."

He let Pfouts pour dust and nuggets into the balanced pan twice, and then pour the gold into a bottle below his counter.

"You own a hide," said Pfouts. "Looks like it'd cut up into nice bedsprings for your cabin bunk." He eyed Aristotle solemnly.

"Better try another. They know I'm going."

"Make nice bags to haul a heavy metal," said Pfouts.

Aristotle stared. "Want to buy eleven good claims, record them later?"

Pfouts beetle-browed that a bit. "Let me think on it. Not for myself. I'm a merchant, but not agin' turning a profit. You peddling your big one, the number twelve, I believe it is?"

"Make an offer," replied Aristotle. The twelfth claim below Fairweather's discovery claim had made him rich.

Aristotle rolled up the hide and stalked into the street, where sharp-eyed loafers lounging against the pillars of store porches observed the man and purchase.

Aristotle bought two pounds of beef, or maybe buffalo, at Gohn and Kohrs, passed the bat-wing doors of the Idaho Club, passed the morc respectable Morier's Saloon, peered down into Daylight Gulch and the rising Virginia City Brewery, and then turned up Alder Gulch to go to his cabin.

Leather, he thought. Harness work tonight, make some tough saddlebags, a pair, able to carry two hundred pounds safely, a hundred on each side.

"Afternoon, Mr. Ives," he said to the grinning blond idler with electric-blue eyes, whose gaze dogged him.

"Afternoon, Scrimshaw," replied George Ives, hitching his pearly-handled artillery. "What you got there?"

"Some future saddlebags," replied Aristotle, climbing the red mud slope toward his cabin.

He felt the sapphire gaze on his back as he climbed through the heatless light.

Chapter Six

Six of them, all coming from the right. On the left, the Beaverhead River gurgled past, thirty yards from the road. Dumb place to try it, he thought. He'd shoot some this time. Gil Train snarled at the horses, yanked up his whip, and laid it over the rumps of the wheelers. The three spans picked up speed, trotting, then loping. Behind them the coach lurched and pounded, hammering Fortitude's tailbone and threatening to heave him off his perch.

Fortitude heard the flat crack of a distant revolver. Let 'em try it, he thought savagely. Hitting a lurching target at a hundred yards with a popgun. More snaps. A horse bloomed red along the withers. It screeched and bucked in harness, dragged on by the others.

"Faster, dammit," he yelled at the driver.

Train glanced at him white-faced and roared at the horses.

Road agents! Fortitude thought, and spit. Wind caught the pearly gob and spun it into his boot. Would this country ever get clear of them? Like a disease, a fever, killing the camps. The coach hit a hole, careened on two wheels, righted itself. He heard shouts from within. Dumb advertisin' miners! he thought. He didn't know which he hated worse, road agents or greenhorns.

All six closed in now, angling from ahead. A bullet spanged from his seat back. He hunkered low, making a small target, and then straightened up, held on the first three, nicely bunched, and squeezed. Two of their horses reared up, spilling riders. Third kept galloping. He centered his scattergun on the man's chest and squeezed again. Chest reddened and the man somersaulted off. Bay horse shrieked. Fortitude set down the first scattergun and lifted the second.

"Load that," he yelled at Train. The driver, with hands full of lines, started to yell back, but didn't.

Fortitude blew the third and fourth shots at the next batch, and scared them off temporarily. He ducked low, jabbed new paper cartridges into all four chambers, and patiently capped four nipples. Two fell off and he had to try again. The remaining road agents had pulled alongside now and were yelling at him, lowering their revolvers at him.

Crouched low in his seat, Fortitude swung the scattergun around, snugged the stock under his arm instead of against his shoulder, and blew it. The recoil rammed the weapon into his ribs. That did it: the bloodied road agents gave up and pulled back.

"Got the bastards," Fortitude snarled. "You can slow 'em down in a bit."

Gil Train whoaed back the horses into a sweated trot and then a steaming walk. They stank of foam and heat, and their sides bellowed. Green scum foamed their crotches.

"Stop the coach, driver," came a cultivated voice from below. That pilgrim.

Gil Train twisted around for a look, and started cursing.

"What's the trouble with him?" barked Fortitude. "He sick or something?"

"No," sighed Train, "he's leaning out the window with a revolver aimed at my back."

"One inside!" Fortitude snarled, and subsided into violent blaspheming of all road agents and their parents.

Wearily, Gil Train halted the coach. Horses snuffed and coughed and pawed earth. The coach rocked under the seat.

The pilgrim, the one in the furry gray suit and string tie, slid to the ground. "Hands up," he said crisply.

"Like hell," yelled Fortitude. "You can get me, but you're dead if you try." He swung his remaining scattergun toward the pilgrim and squeezed. The explosion shattered the silence, making horses jerk in their harness. Pilgrim's chest bloomed red and he sagged to earth, coughing once. His blue revolver belched.

Too late. The others had him covered from three mounts now. All of them showed blood where Fortitude's shot had hit home.

"Drop it, Hayes," said one silkily from behind his yellow face mask. The voice sounded familiar.

Hayes had one barrel left, but he lowered it. Let them clean out the Hibernians, he thought. Served the freckleheads right.

"Might kill you, Hayes. Three of the boys are hurt bad. And this one"—he toed the corpse—"looks mortuaried."

"Do it good," Hayes whispered. "Do it good because my last act will be to blow my last barrel into you."

Yellow-mask laughed shortly, but lowered the bore of his big Walker Colt slightly. He slid off his bloodied scarified sorrel and yanked the coach door open.

"Out, gents," he said.

"We're just broke miners, me lads," sang one. "Haven't got a shilling."

"Out."

Fortitude felt the coach sway under him as heavy weight shifted. He lowered his hands a few notches.

"Keep 'em high, Hayes," yelled one on horseback. A kid. A kid's scared voice under that yellow hood.

The red-faced miners clambered to the grass and stood.

"Take what ya will. We just got a few poor ounces to send back home to our starvin' families. Take it all," said the talkative one. "Here, lads, I'll toss my poke."

"Slow," commanded the road agent.

"I hate to do it, Mike. It's for my mither. Must I do it?" asked the middle one, the tenor one.

The road agent fired into the dirt, a terrible startling crack that plowed lead inches from the middle of one's boots.

Fortitude watched patiently. He'd seen all this before, more times than he cared to think about. If the miners obeyed, they'd probably live to tell about it. Instant death otherwise.

The shot hastened them. Each drew out a small soft-leather poke with tight drawstrings and tossed it to earth. The road agent hefted each and laughed.

"Drop your pants, Micks," he said.

"What air you talkin' about?"

This time the shot burned through suit-coat cloth, tugging at that one's arm.

"You've ruint my suit!" he exclaimed.

"If I have to tell you again, you're dead," said the robber silkily. Fortitude tried to place that voice.

Reluctantly the miners lowered their britches. One undid a belt; the other two pulled off worsted black suit coats and then lowered galluses, until suit pants slithered down chalky white legs and gathered around squeaky new shoes.

The agents laughed. Suspended from thongs tied around their middles were heavy black pokes, looking like oversized private parts.

"Why, ain't they the bulls," said one, smirking. "For your old mither across the sea, was it?"

The boy outlaw laughed nastily. Skinny kid with albino hair, almost. Maybe light blond, Fortitude thought. Easy enough to spot unless it was a wig, which it might well be. He studied the hairs on the kid's hands. No color at all. Just hairs.

"Untie your privates, boys," said the agent.

"It's all I got in the world," moaned one of them, the one who'd stayed silent. "Would you be leaving us a bit to start over?"

The agents laughed. As the heavy pokes fell to earth, one agent picked them up, hefted them, then opened up the drawstrings for a look. He nodded to the others. "It ain't gravel," he said. "Hate to go to all this trouble for river gravel."

He stared up at Train. "You. Get going. Your passengers are staying here awhile to take the air and see the elephant."

"But—" began Gil. "You've got their pokes. We'll just—"

"Get the hell out of here before I shoot."

Fortitude rested a hand on Gil's arm, a signal.

"You. Hayes. I ought to kill you."

"Try it," snarled Fortitude.

Trembling visibly, Gil Train snapped the lines over the horses. The bleeding one on the off side of the middle span had quieted. A flesh wound, a furrow. The horses lowered into their harness and pulled, lifting the coach into motion. Fortitude kept his hands halfway up, and his back itched. He did not look around for a while. At a hundred yards, he looked around. The three miners, pants still snarled around ankles, were being prodded and herded toward the river.

"Think they'll live?" asked Gil tightly.

"Some say a hundred, some say two hundred missing," replied Fortitude angrily. "Dead men don't talk. Irish dead men with no ties over here don't have families, either."

He felt pity for them. They'd probably be shot in the back and dumped in the Beaverhead, fish food to the Missouri River and beyond. They'd come five thousand miles to escape grinding famine and bad times. Left behind mothers and paps, ribby brothers and sisters, stone cottages too full of life, come to get ahead in a land of promise, send a little coin back. Just get ahead somehow, hard work, army fodder—the whole damned Union Army was Irish, he thought. Get ahead, get dead.

"Why not us?" muttered Gil. "I know, but I always ask it anyway. Why not me?"

Because they were more or less immune. Shoot drivers and shotgun messengers enough and the coaches would quit coming. Shoot teamsters enough and the freight wagons would stop. These camps hung on those lifelines. Kiskadden, Oliver, Caldwell and the rest of the owners had all gotten word out. Leave their men alone or the wagons and coaches would pinch off and there'd be nothing. No potatoes.

Train walked the tired horses to Dempsey's stop, four miles ahead, and all the while Fortitude raged. Spies everywhere. Even in the coaches. Spies to tell them who to target, who hid gold in his britches. Who would blab about Scrimshaw's fool's coach?

Wearily Randolph Figaro turned over the two cards, the jack of diamonds the loser, the seven of clubs the winner. On the green oilcloth lay a stack of ten chips, dollar chips, on the spade seven.

Figaro's lithe fingers slid chips from his faro bank and matched the stack on the oilcloth. Then his swift fingers adjusted the cases on the abacuslike contraption beside him to show that the jack and seven had been played and were in the discard pile. Players kept track, guessing at which of the cards remaining in the deck would come up.

The young man across from him pulled his winning stack off the gaming layout area and slid the other stack to the eight. The deck had thinned to a few cards and only one eight had appeared. He grinned at Professor Figaro, a blinding, triumphant grin.

"You're going to lose, professor," he said.

"Looks like it, George." He found himself peering at those dazzling blue eyes, eyes that ushered any careful observer into a kind of happy madness of the soul behind them. How could one pair of ice-blue eyes, set in a sculptured, lean head with a shock of sunny blond hair on it, convey such wild contradiction? Menace, frost, heat, amusement, murder? Tonight George Ives seemed more, more of everything. More taut, more amiable, more vicious, more comic, more friendly . . . and more deadly. Everything intensified, as if seen through opium smoke.

Maybe that was it, Figaro thought. Opium. But he knew it wasn't so. No man patronizing Churchill's Saloon stayed more sober and alert. On this Wednesday night the place seemed empty. No one else sported at his table. A poker game proceeded under blue haze in a lamplit corner, and two hard men downed red-eye at the bar, one after another. For that matter, Figaro wondered, how did anyone know it was Wednesday? It could be Monday or Sunday. What was time and date in a mining camp?

George Ives answered that for him. "The sheriff's become impatient," he said, sliding chips out again. "You came to a little understanding with him about dealing here at Churchill's. Nice place to deal, I'd say. But, professor, you're reneging."

Figaro forced himself to stay casual. "Oh," he murmured. "I forgot. Something about having the house keep accounts, was it?"

George Ives grinned. "Something like that."

How could anyone not like this blond youth full of such boyish charm? thought the professor. So diffident—and yet so commanding. The slightest suggestion voiced by this young man before him became orders for a host of hard men. In the weeks Randolph Figaro had dealt faro here, he'd seen men leap to perform anything George Ives casually wished. Let him wish a cigar, and a rough, unkempt man would hasten to the bar and get one from Churchill. Let George Ives inquire whose horses were tied to the hitch rails of the bakery, or either of the mercantiles, or Morier's Saloon, and two men would leap out the door, rain, snow, or cold, and eventually report back, while Ives's wild eyes flared their odd fires. Let Sheriff Plummer ride over from Bannack City for some entertainments in the new camp, and George Ives would be at his elbow. Not even his deputies Jack Gallagher, Ned Ray, and Buck Stinson commanded the sheriff's time as much as the sunny young Adonis across from him. It said something about George Ives, he thought.

"I had forgotten," said the gambler. "Do you suppose this place is quite safe for my bank? My winnings feel safer to me locked in Dance's safe. Or maybe I should try Elling's new bank when it opens."

He met Ives's mad blue eyes steadily.

A six and an eight, loser, winner.

"See how you've won, George. Cleaning me tonight." He

shoved another stack of dollar tokens across the oilcloth. The cloth showed bare thread in places, he noted. He'd get another. It didn't do for a sporting man to use a tattered layout.

"You have nice gentle fingers," said Ives brightly. "Tools of your trade, I suppose. Yes, gamblers need fingers and hands, fingers to hold cards, fingers to deal, deal swift and light, faster than the eye. Oh, yes, people in your profession need fingers and hands."

Professor Figaro swiftly got the thrust of this. He'd dreaded something like this, their next step. He'd barely slept for five days for fear of being murdered in his cot in the back of Churchill's. He'd scarcely left the place, and then only to take his meals at Dale's Eats up on Wallace. To leave was to invite a tail or two. He'd stayed away from Dance's, too, and had kept his winnings in a poke in his pocket.

"Maybe you should copper your bet this time, George. Five or six cards left; two eights. Maybe one's the hock. People forget about the hock."

"Soft white hands," said George. "I'd hate to see anything happen to them. Destroy your living the rest of your life. Maybe there will be an accident."

"Not in Churchill's," said Randolph. "This is a friendly place, and I'm a friend. You're a friend." He smiled his long saturnine toothy smile. Randolph Figaro's smile lay crooked over his mouth. A gambler's smile, he had thought, observing it in many a looking glass. Something to put others ill at ease. Smile crooked and play a square game. That worked better than smiling saintly and bracing decks.

Some wild light flailed from Ives's eyes like sapphires in sun. "We're like a little private club here. We help each other out. We know each other, too. We're all together. All except you. The sheriff was just being pals, inviting you into our club."

Mad azure flame licked his pupils. A phenomenon, Professor Figaro thought. The man had gas jets burning in his skull.

He turned over two eights, loser and winner. Lazily he raked in George Ives's chips.

"There, you see, George. Eights can be dangerous," he said softly.

"I'm cleaned out. Perhaps you'll lend me five thousand, professor. Five thousand before sundown tomorrow. I'll pick it up from Churchill."

Randolph Figaro didn't answer. He adjusted the cases, pulled the deck out of the casebox, shuffled, and waited for new sports.

Ives rose abruptly, grinned boyishly, and wandered off, clapping the hardcases at the plank bar amiably. Randolph Figaro fanned out the deck on the table and eased back into the stone wall behind him, his hooded eyes studying the place.

How did they know that Figaro had exactly five thousand in nuggets and dust in Dance's safe? Remarkable. Eyes and ears. The dour bootblack, of course. Several times Lane had slithered in here, whispered something, and left. Randolph Figaro saw that and more, most every day. He knew who the road agents were, give or take a few. He knew who their allies and small fry and errand boys were. He knew too much, enough to get him killed. Enough to lose his bank. Enough to get his fingers mashed to pulp. He wasn't sure whether they would simply steal his bank from him and then kill him, or whether it would be, as Plummer proposed, a surety, a bond, guaranteeing his silence and loyalty.

He rolled that over in his mind, sucking on a cigarillo. Not a surety. He knew too much and they meant to kill him—after he coughed up his gold from Dance's safe. He had run out of time. The ride he'd been promised by Hayes hadn't materialized. The old shotgun messenger had slid onto the bench beside him at Dale's Eats, looked about at half a dozen others—one of whom, Figaro knew, kept tabs on the gambler—and whispered two or three cryptic things: "Armed coach leaving shortly for Fort Hall or Salt Lake. Night trip. Be ready on ten minutes' notice."

"How?" Figaro had whispered.

"Three taps on your storeroom window from outside."

"What if I'm playing in the saloon?"

"Then you miss the ride. But it'll be after midnight. After the saloon usually closes."

Hayes had slid off the bench, and that was the last Randolph saw of him. The gambler glanced covertly at the bum who always trailed him, wondering if he'd heard. But he'd come to a swift decision: he'd simply leave the dust in Dance's safe and flee with whatever he had with him, his working cash of about five hundred in dust and greenbacks, and his winnings in these days of waiting. Dance seemed honest enough and the gold would be safe enough—for a while. He knew mining camps. A year in one seemed like a decade anywhere else. Things changed. Bandits and crooks rose and fell. Law and order always came, one way or another. . . . The dust at Dance's could wait. Unless Dance sold out. . . .

He sat idly, thinking about George Ives, the road agents' top man in the camp. The remembrance of those wild azure eyes chilled him. He had perhaps twenty hours to live. Turn over his bank and they'd kill him. Keep his bank in Dance's and they'd kill him too. No ride. No place to hide. He knew then what he'd do. If the three taps didn't come tonight, he'd flee sometime in the small hours. Take his layout if he could fold it up silently and slip past the two or three toughs always sleeping somewhere in the saloon. No way out except through the creaking plank door in front. And once he got out into the frosty night, no place to go. He didn't know where Hayes lived. He didn't know who his travel companions would be. He wouldn't dare show up at Peabody and Caldwell, looking for Hayes. He didn't know anything except that he'd likely be dead if he cowered in Churchill's Saloon.

Well, he thought, he'd always been a gambling man.

Chapter Seven

Tonight.

The reality of it gnawed at Aristotle Scrimshaw. Tonight they'd leave. Tonight they'd make a desperate run with a battered coach through hundreds of miles of bandit-infested wilderness. He might die. He might lose his gold. He might never see dear Annette and his children again.

Last night he slipped down to the Peabody and Caldwell yards to finish mending harness, and deep in the silent moon-silvered night Fortitude Hayes materialized.

"Get your gold out of Dance's somehow," Fortitude said. "Tomorrow we roll. Creed's ready and says the moon's right; he can see the road just fine. He's feeling fit as a bull moose."

"Tomorrow?" muttered Aristotle. "But—I haven't had a chance to sell my claims. I've got a saddlebag to finish—that's hard work, cutting leather and riveting it. And—"

"Tomorrow!" snapped Fortitude. "The longer we wait, the more people know. Creed's a good man but a blabber. How's this harness? You got it together? We gonna hafta borrow good harness and make everyone mad around here?"

"I've got everything but the breeching for the wheelers."

Hayes squinted at him in the silver light. "This thing got brakes?"

They clambered up on the repaired coach and looked. No brakes, shaft broken.

"I'll rig some breeching from rope," muttered Aristotle. So little time and so many details.

For an hour, they whispered plans. Hayes had to get word to Angelica over in Bannack City, and to Professor Figaro. There'd be no waiting. If the others weren't notified or ready, they'd be left behind. Everything depended on speed, getting down to Fort Hall before the road agents got word and got organized.

"They got me coming back, near Dempsey's, broad daylight, too. Pulled some miners off the coach and we'll never see them again."

"Murder," whispered Aristotle, his stomach lurching. If they'd murder miners for a small poke or two, what would they do to him, with four hundred pounds of dust and nuggets?

"You scared?"

"Yes, I'm scared. I've never been so scared."

Fortitude slapped him on the back. "Good. I found out something in the war. Scared men soldiered better. Give me some good and scared men, not a cocky bastard in the bunch, and they'd fight."

They stared quietly at the black hulk of the coach, wondering about it.

"I wish we could test this first," said Aristotle.

"Since we can't, let's go over it," replied Fortitude.

They studied it minutely, spun wheels, checked axles and trees, ran harness from it, examined leather, rigged a makeshift seat in the empty coach, and pronounced it fit.

"Be here at one. Creed and I'll have the team harnessed. I'll tap on Figaro's window and hope he makes it. I'll send a coded message to the lady in Bannack in the morning."

"And my gold?" asked Aristotle softly.

"That's a problem for you to figure out. If I side you when you get it out, they'll know Caldwell and Peabody are involved."

That's how they'd left it. Each man slid into the night, watching the moon shadows with heart-stabbing fear.

Aristotle didn't sleep much in his miner's cabin. His mind worked compulsively through the night until he lay haggard by dawn. He rose early, tried to down an oatmeal breakfast and couldn't, and waited fretfully until Paris Pfouts opened his emporium.

In the space of an hour, Aristotle deeded all his eleven claims to Paris, who agreed to share the resale profits fifty-fifty and forward money to Scrimshaw in Wisconsin. Then Aristotle borrowed Pfouts's dray and wagon, harnessed up, and waited. His plan was simple enough: wait for a moment when George Lane, road agent spy, wasn't in Dance and Stuart's, get his pokes from Walter Dance, load them into a cast-iron stove he would appear to be buying, and drive off with a cast-iron stove full of gold. The other clerk, Wilburforce, might or might not blab to Lane later. Dance wouldn't.

It turned out to be a long, miserable wait under a cold, brassy sun. Aristotle nursed coffee in Dale's Eats, at a window seat that gave him a view of Dance and Stuart's emporium up Wallace and across the street. Outside, the dray flicked its tail and waited, head down. Twice Aristotle wandered in, noted Lane industriously blacking boots, keeping a malevolent eye on the small green safe and on Aristotle. But the other clerk, Wilburforce, was nowhere in sight.

"Walter," he said in a voice that sounded strange in his throat, "how much is that stove? I want something better to winter with."

Dance stared at him sulfurously. "Fifty-seven dollars. Seventeen for the stove, forty for shipping it here, and that's a bargain since they usually want a dollar a pound."

"Seems high," muttered Aristotle. "Everything's high. I'll bring a wagon over later. Will you or Lane there help me slide the stove on?"

The back door of Dance's store formed a raised loading dock at wagon-bed height.

"I thought you were leaving town, Scrimshaw," said Lane boldly.

Aristotle didn't answer. "Will you help me load the stove, Lane? In an hour or two?"

"Can't say as I'll be here."

"I'll be back with a wagon, Walter," Aristotle said. He returned into the sun-bleached street, noting the scabrous loafers and informants lounging on wooden porches as they always did, even on cold days. Small-fry who reported everything to Ives or whoever was above Ives, Aristotle thought. No one ever said it; to whisper it was to invite death. But somehow miners knew, by some sort of osmosis, who the road agents and their allies were. They idled their days away, watching miners and businessmen with mocking, insolent eyes, making a small living by supplying information. Aristotle felt their gaze probing him, stabbing him, wounding him as he made his way back to Dale's. The taut hours dragged by. Dance stalked up the hill for lunch. Aristotle began to wonder if the whole scheme would go awry and his escape would be doomed. Dance dawdled back from lunch and a siesta. Stiffly Aristotle abandoned his vigil and walked up Wallace, peering at last into Dance's store. No Lane. Dance lounged alone behind his plank counter.

The sight galvanized Aristotle. He mounted the wagon seat and snapped the old dray into a lethargic walk to the alley behind Dance's.

Dry-mouthed, Aristotle stalked into the dark, musk-scented confines of the store. "I'll take the stove. And two lengths of stovepipe. And get my gold out of your safe," he rasped from a parched throat. "Hurry! Hurry, Walter!"

Dance peered disdainfully at him. "Now whoa up. You owe me storage charges on all them pokes. We'll just figure this out good and proper. Every poke's got a start-up date for charges. Now I'll jist start adding, young man."

"Let me load the stove while you wait."

"That ain't businesslike. You can load after your stove's bought and paid for and I get the charges added up."

Wildly Aristotle waited while Dance scratched figures out on foolscap with a nib pen. Twice he was interrupted by customers, one of them a cadaverous punk, one of Virginia City's drunks. The man's oily gaze settled on Aristotle while Dance sold him a nickel cigar.

Never had Aristotle Scrimshaw felt such rage toward an ordinary merchant as he felt toward Dance, while the proprietor phlegmatically waited on customers and totted up figures.

"Comes to a hundred thirty-seven dollars, with the stove," he announced at last.

"A hundred thirty-seven dollars!"

"Kept your pokes safe for months, Scrimshaw." Dance stared back at him imperiously.

"Banks treat customers a lot better."

Dance shrugged.

Tautly Aristotle dragged the heavy stove to the loading platform and onto the wagon bed, staring viciously up and down the alley. Then he jammed pokes of gold into it—a fortune in gold—until all thirty-four pokes nestled in the cast-iron belly, the last poke considerably lightened by Dance's extravagant charges.

Aristotle slammed the stove door shut, glared around, feeling a thousand eyes watching him from rooftops, slitted windows, and street corners. But in fact the alley lay silent in the cold sun of late afternoon.

He didn't feel like good-byes to Dance, so he clambered up on his wagon seat, pulled his oiled and reloaded Navy out of its holster and set it beside him, and hawed the old dray. He felt naked. He felt on the brink of death. He felt spied upon. But as he turned from Van Buren onto Wallace, he spotted nothing unusual. Loafers' eyes did notice him, as they always did, did study the cast iron stove and stovepipe thoughtfully, did note that Scrimshaw turned off Wallace in the direction of his cabin and his claims, and then gazed elsewhere.

Within minutes, Aristotle knew, the road agents would learn

that Scrimshaw had purchased a cast-iron stove from Dance and had hauled it to his cabin using Pfouts's dray and wagon.

Back at his claim he parked the wagon in front of his cabin and unharnessed the dray and set it to grazing on a picket line. A magpie exploded from a nearby alder, startling Aristotle into clawing for his Navy Colt. Inside his cabin, he edged down beside the open door with frayed nerves and waited for night, his muscles and mind taut. He felt exhausted, and yet the ordeal had barely begun. Just outside his door, in a weathered gray wagon, squatted an ugly black stove with four hundred pounds of dust and nuggets in it. Just for whimsy's sake, Aristotle jammed a section of shiny blue stovepipe over thc flange of the stove. That would be his ensign, the erect stovepipe, the sign of his black defiancc of a murderous band of road agents, some of whom were no doubt peering at his wagon and his stove and his handiwork right now from the heights above Alder Gulch. He sat down just inside his door and waited through the afternoon, slit-eyed.

Professor Figaro dozed in his corner, or appeared to. Actually, he coldly calculated his chances in the smoky amber haze of Churchill's. He eased his silver turnip watch from his brocaded gray watershot silk vest. Almost midnight, sun time. They went by local time here, same as everywhere else. Pfouts had rigged a pole in front of his stone-and-adobe-mortar store and had made a mark on the storefront denoting true south. When the shadow of the pole lay squarely on the mark, it was noon.

He'd fold his layout at midnight and wait an hour in the storeroom for the three taps. If they didn't come, he'd slip out into the night—somewhere. He eyed his old faro layout dolefully. Two hundred in Lincoln's skins—he'd bought it from a busted sporting man and paid more than it was worth. It'd be hard to replace, except in Denver City. He had bank enough, but finding another faro layout in the untracked West would tax him. He'd lose this one . . . unless he could sneak it out with him.

He thought Churchill might close, and stared covertly at the choleric blocky barkeep, who looked bored sitting dourly behind his raw plank bar. Four rough, bearded men in greasy britches and worn shirts played sloppy poker in the wavering light of an untrimmed lamp that smoked. They were all loosened by red-eye. Churchill's hooded gaze flicked around the silent room, glanced off Figaro, and retreated back to his jugs. He'd scarcely spoken to the gambler ever since Plummer and Ives had started the squeeze. Still, the saloonkeeper didn't shut down. Figaro yawned, thinking to fold up and wait in his tiny room for whatever would come in the next hour. His nerves shouted at him, and he felt the tic that spasmed his eyelid begin twitching again. It happened more and more, and he couldn't control it. In poker it worked to his advantage because the others observed it and thought he held cards or bluffed.

Outside, he heard the footfall of horses and the hoarse camaraderie of mocking men. Moments later Churchill's came alive as whooping rough men boiled in, crowded the plank bar, and ordered good whiskey—a sign of successful plunder. He knew them all and watched tensely as they settled down to serious drinking. George Ives tossed back a rare drink, his electric eyes flaring and lancing, jabbing briefly at Figaro with some luminous fire. The professor felt the jolt of them, and sensed that time had run out. Whatever fate dealt to him would happen in moments.

A few, such as Boone Helm and Whiskey Bill Graves and Ned Ray, remained dour and alert. But the younger bucks, Bob Zachary, Frank Parish, Haze Lyons, Alec Carter, and the rest, were making a woolly night of it. Figaro sensed murder; sometime soon Ives would start something deadly.

Zachary and Steve Marshland settled on stools in front of the professor's layout.

"Test the luck again, perfesser," said Marshland. "Easy come, easy go."

Figaro weighed good-quality dust, slid it into his bank poke, and pushed grimy blue chips to both of them. He shuffled the deck ritually, turned over the soda, a low club, and began to deal. They bet lightly at first, waiting to see the cases.

"Luck of the Irish," said Zachary. "I got the luck of the Irish tonight."

Randolph Figaro played automatically, winning and losing, keeping cases by rote, scarcely aware of the game for once. Covertly he studied Ives, who stood with his back against the bar, his body charged with some wild tension, radiating that curious mixture of murder and humor that Figaro had come to understand. Murder had become some kind of comic orgasm in Ives, and the closer Ives edged toward it, the more he grinned. Tonight Ives chortled and chuckled and grinned.

"Hey, I won, perfesser. You forgot to pay me," said Steve Marshland.

Jolted back to his game, Figaro paid out chips on Marshland's coppered king.

"Sorry, Steve," he said. "I was just enjoying the revelry around here."

Churchill had been expecting this crowd, stayed open for this celebration, and now carefully avoided glancing in the professor's direction. They all ignored Figaro except Ives.

"I'm taking a little break, gents. Call of nature. Game continues in five."

He stood, wondering how smart they were. Few professional gamblers ever left their tables, and all gamblers possessed an iron discipline over their bodies. Ritually, he kept the cases for the last play, a seven of hearts and jack of diamonds, and walked tautly to his room.

Now or never. The quiet stone cubicle seemed a safe place in the yellow candlelight. But it wasn't. He would walk into the night this very moment if they'd let him. He wanted his greatcoat but didn't dare. Taking it would be a giveaway. But his dark swallowtail with the chesterfield collar wouldn't be much against November cold. Trembling, he slid two new decks of cards—his livelihood—into a breast pocket. Into a generous hip pocket he slid spare ammunition for his hideout revolver. Nothing for his derringer. He yearned to take his few things, spare linens, spare patent leather shoes, silk hat, walking stick with spring-loaded dagger in its base, the tintype . . . the locket. Yes, those. He had to take those, the small links to a lost past, to his parents and a woman he'd loved.

With fingers that scarcely worked, he opened the filagreed silver locket and beheld her, Amanda, frozen on porcelain at twenty, lustrous brown sausage curls, wide hazel eyes, pouty lips, a broad naked expanse of neck and chest. At the rise of her breasts the miniature stopped, but he knew she'd posed in a green watershot silk dress for the Natchez portraitist. The wife of his youth, dead now.

He slid the locket into his pocket with the spare balls and caps, added the small tintype of his long-gone parents—his only links to his past, to a life more honorable than the one he had come to know—and blew out the candle.

Churchill's had no rear door and no outhouse. Customers walked out the front door, wended their way to the rear of the building, and wet its stone wall. Now, wearing exactly what he had been wearing, Randolph Figaro jerked spastically through the hazy saloon, feeling Ives's mad blue eyes following him step by step along the bar, among roistering men, step by step past Churchill and his jugs and bottles, to the rough plank door. No one stopped him. The shout or shot didn't come.

He saw Ives glance at Zachary and Marshland, take in the idle faro layout, and relax. Then Figaro stepped into a bitter cold and black night. Before him a dozen horses lined the hitch rail, hipshot and dozing. Above him a pale moon hung in a silvered heaven. Virginia City had no streetlights. Its saloons and hostelries had long since extinguished their lamps. Cover Street lay black before him. He paused, listening for the footfall of thugs, hearing nothing.

He didn't know where to go. If Hayes had tried to reach him, tap on his small window, he'd missed it when the midnight crowd roared in and kept him at his game. It pierced him that he walked utterly alone now. No miners or respectable men trusted him because he had set up at Churchill's. If Hayes and his coach had left, he had missed his chance. He would be too ill-dressed to survive in wilderness, hide out by day and walk by night. Not in November. And when they realized he'd slipped out, they'd come after him, and then he'd be as good as dead. Well, he thought, he'd always been a gambler. Only now, the stakes couldn't be higher.

He edged upslope toward Wallace Street and found it as inky as Cover. Cold bit at him. No gloves, no hat. The enormity of what he was doing hit him hard. His eyes had adjusted now, and he made out the black hulks of buildings lining Wallace Street. And something else. Far down the street, a faint orange light. He felt drawn to it, moth to flame, a false haven. He stepped lightly along the rutted street, clinging to shadow. Morier's. The first saloon in Virginia City, and a respectable one. Maybe he could beg a corner there to sleep in. . . .

He pulled open the rough door and stared at two startled men, who gaped at the unexpected intrusion. The barkeep, balding and massive, in a soiled white apron, and an even more massive man, a veritable giant flamboyantly dressed in blue wool shirt, huge black belt, wide-brimmed felt hat. Tucked into his belt were gauntlets. He stared arrogantly at Figaro from startled small eyes set beside a thick curved nose, and smiled faintly.

Randolph Figaro couldn't quite place him, but the man wore the insignia of his trade. He would be a Jehu, a stagecoach driver.

"Whiskey," croaked Figaro. The barkeep poured silently, and then the three men stared at one another, no one speaking.

Chapter Eight

Calvin Creed relished the moment and relished the night. He considered himself the best Jehu in the business. No one else had his ways with horses, could string three or even four spans of horses around a hairpin mountain curve without tangling them all up. The more menacing the road agents, the better he liked it. Tonight he'd start a trip he could brag about for years.

He guzzled beer at Morier's, bragging and waiting. Hayes and Scrimshaw had long since slipped down to the stage yards and harnessed the three spans in the repaired gear. Creed had watched Scrimshaw do it. He'd make Scrimshaw change teams the whole trip. No self-respecting Jehu of Creed's caliber would stoop to such yardwork. Like a ship's captain, he'd run this show, set the starting time—he was in no hurry at all—decide what to do, when to rest, when to run. Hayes had told him the whole thing: a half ton of gold to slide by those road agents! He itched to tell the bandits the time and place, just so he could enjoy a war and a run, but he didn't. Instead he hinted broadly to friendly and unfriendly ears that a big load, a treasure, would pull out soon. Everyone knew about Scrimshaw's treasure in Dance's safe—and it tickled him that he'd be hauling an even larger one, Angelica's, along with it.

Scrimshaw had been jumpy as a hare at the darkened yard. He pulled in with Pfouts's wagon soon after dusk, itchy and nervous, reins in one hand, Navy Colt in the other. Quietly he and Hayes had pulled pokes out of the stove and settled them into the four leather pockets of two crude mochila saddlebags, a hundred pounds per pocket. Then they'd simply riveted the pockets shut, sealing the gold in the saddlebags. They'd wrestled the heavy saddlebags into the seatless belly of the coach, put Pfouts's dray into the corrals—the merchant would pick up horse and wagon in the morning—and settled down to wait in the blackness.

Creed had strolled over to Wallace Street to sluice beer and boast—he had no intention of leaving until around two in the morning, which would put him at Daly's about daybreak. They'd change teams there in the dawn light and not have to track down wild cayuses in the dark. After midnight Hayes had slipped over to Churchill's Saloon and tapped on Figaro's small window. And that was it. Meanwhile, Creed had some drinking to do. He cut a splendid figure, thick and massive and contemptuous of the world, and wanted to show off a bit while the clock ticked. He'd put on a new navy-blue flannel shirt over long johns, strapped his black twill britches in place with a massive flared and silver-studded black belt, tied a light blue kerchief around his neck, and tucked huge wolf-fur-trimmed roughout leather gauntlets into his belt, with the woolen gloves inside them. He wore his wide-brimmed gray felt hat pushed forward to shadow his granite face.

For two hours he'd regaled the denizens of Morier's with tales of road agents, escapes, derring-do, and death, plus a hint or two of a treasure the bandits would miss. At last only Morier remained, dutifully pouring suds into Creed's empty mug—until Randolph Figaro stepped in, looking wild and distraught.

"Professor Figaro," said Creed. A statement, not a question. Calvin Creed never asked questions.

Figaro nodded.

"Wandering around late. They close up Churchill's?"

The pasty-faced professor glanced first at Morier, then at Creed. "Not yet," he muttered.

"Who's there—at Churchill's?"

Figaro shrugged. "Who isn't there?"

"Pretty late for such a large crowd."

"They all came in awhile ago," Figaro said.

Creed laughed. Hayes had told him about yesterday morning's holdup. "They had something to celebrate," he said. "But the joke's on them."

Figaro nodded, puzzled, and sipped his drink shakily. "I don't believe we've met," he said, his liquid gaze probing.

"Calvin Creed."

The name rang no bells with the gambler, and Creed felt annoyed. "Most people know me and my trade."

"I know your trade," replied Figaro. "You wear it like a flag."

"Friend of Fortitude Hayes—same company . . . same trips, same ideas about road agents."

Some obscure excitement lit the gambler's face. "Could you take me to him? Now?"

"Just heading thataway. Come along, friend." He drained the last of the sour beer and smacked the mug down on Morier's planks.

With alacrity, the gambler tagged along as Creed bulled through the door into the icy night. Behind them, Morier snuffed the lamp, looking relieved.

"How come you to Morier's?" boomed Creed, oblivious of danger in the night.

"Sheer luck," whispered Figaro, squinting into the shadows.

"Don't need to whisper, man. No hooligan takes on Calvin Creed."

But Figaro whispered anyway, and in a few moments Creed had the gambler's story and knew how the desperate flight ended in Morier's saloon.

"Hayes didn't reach you, then," Creed boomed.

"I was out at my layout. If he came, I missed him."

"No matter. We'll be off directly."

The moon lay high and silvery, and in its bleak, cold light Creed saw the battered coach, hulking harnessed and ready. Canvas had been stretched over the bashed-in side. Hayes and Scrimshaw watched Creed and Figaro come, and Creed caught the glint of silvery light on black barrels. The young miner glared at the gambler, not liking the sight of swallowtail coat and watershot silk and the tinhorn's morose face. If the professor noticed Scrimshaw's flinty distrust, he ignored it.

No one spoke. The Jehu pulled on woolen gloves and then the gauntlets. He studied the teams, tugged harness, snorted at the hemp ropes that served as breeching over the rumps of the wheelers. He peered into the shadowed bowels of the coach.

"No seats. You'll bounce around like Mex jumping beans," he said to Figaro and Scrimshaw.

The young miner nodded.

"How we armed, Fortitude?"

"I'll have two double-barreled shotguns. And I got the spare from the office. They'll have that in the coach, plus their own sidearms."

"These gents paid their fare?"

"Not yet. Sixty apiece for your persons. Four hundred pounds of gold times twenty cents to Fort Hall is eighty dollars for freight, Scrimshaw."

In the stage office they quietly weighed dust by moonlight, and Hayes jammed it into the company strongbox.

"We got any robes in here, Fortitude?" asked Creed. Briefly he described Figaro's flight into the night.

"That cut it close, professor. But it all came together. Sure, we got robes here."

He rummaged around, found two old buffalo robes kept for drivers and shotgun messengers riding in cold weather, and stowed them in the black hold.

"Let's go, then," said Creed. He walked smartly to the hulking coach, savoring it all, and clambered up to the driver's seat, settling himself on the off side. Hayes gimped up and joined him on the near side, hefting his shotgun. Beneath them the coach rocked, and they heard the door close on the side that still had a door. The coach leaned slightly to the left.

Creed didn't like it. "You and Scrimshaw check that thoroughbrace?" he asked the shotgun messenger.

"Looked all right," Fortitude replied shortly.

"Feels wrong."

"Too late to worry about it."

"All aboard, gents," Creed bawled much too loud, but he didn't care.

"Hafta do that?" Hayes growled.

"They're drunk at Churchill's."

"Not all," said Hayes. "Never all."

"Well, then we'll blow the hell out of them," Creed said, snapping lines. He was a virtuoso and sent messages down the long strands of leather, messages that told four-footed beasts to shape up and trot out, to ease up, to rest, to explode into a gallop, to veer around boulders and potholes and mud sinks on a road that scarcely existed through a trackless waste.

He guffawed and set the six horses to trotting smartly. Beneath him the eleven-passenger Concord coach creaked and swayed. They rattled out of the coach yard, down into Alder Gulch, and along the moon-gilded path to Nevada City, Junction, Laurin, and Daly's—where they'd switch teams and hope the outlaws who hung about there would be still asleep.

The coach clattered over frost-glazed stone and mud, the rattle of its passage echoing off dark shanties and tents along the gulch, disturbing the sleep of miners. The coach felt wrong beneath him, swaying oddly, too loosely on the leather thoroughbraces that suspended the coach and insulated both passengers and the team ahead of him from severe jolting. Hayes glared at every shadow, swinging his shotgun at shadows, taut and angry. Creed grinned. Road agents had never struck so close to Virginia City or Nevada City. But he peered around himself, noting the wobble of the off rear wheel, a five-foot-one-inch giant. The smaller front wheels turned smoothly beneath him.

"Easy trip if this wreck lasts," said Creed.

"They'll find us," muttered Hayes. "Learn about us at Daly's. See us change teams in broad daylight at Bunton's—the worst nest of all. See us pick up Angelica and her treasure by broad daylight in Bannack City. And then we've got a long run down to Fort Hall. Four days and nights, Cal."

Creed guffawed. "They ain't organized. They got to have advance knowledge of a shipment to get road agents together."

Hayes muttered, said nothing, squinted into a latticed, leafless glade of alders.

"I ever tell you why they call us drivers Jehus?" said Creed, knowing he'd imparted this bit of knowledge in Hayes's ear about fifty times.

Fortitude didn't reply.

"It's in the Good Book, Second Kings. It says in there—it says, 'And the driving is like the driving of Jehu the son of Nimshi: for he driveth furiously.'"

Calvin Creed bawled out his thick pleasure into the icy hollowness of night.

Below Adobetown, Alder Gulch widened out into a broad flat running between naked humped hills. In only a few miles, the violent jolting of the Concord had bruised Aristotle and set him to yearning for the cushioned seats. The creak and groan of the rumbling coach seemed thunderous in the blackness, enough to awaken anyone for miles around, he thought.

In spite of the frosty air, he rolled up the canvas window cover and peered behind, studying the frosty ruts behind them as they bumped along through sagebrush. He supposed Hayes would be looking, too—that was his job—but Aristotle intended to do his own looking. Beside him the gambler sagged mutely under a heavy buffalo robe, too exhausted to talk. Aristotle eyed him suspiciously, keeping his revolver in hand beneath his robe, ready to disarm the tinhorn, the sporting man, the lowlife, the road agents' ally who'd wormed his way into this coach. But the gambler dozed, or appeared to, and as the minutes ticked by, Aristotle began to study the world passing by the windows—but never for long, and always with sharp covert glances at the gambler.

A horseman. Aristotle couldn't be sure at first. Simply some subtle movement far behind. He peered out the window, studying it, feeling icy air eddy about his head, hearing the rhythmic chatter of the three spans of horses, hearing Creed hawk and spit.

Yes, a horseman, coming fast in a controlled mile-eating lope, gaining swiftly on the trotting teams of coach horses.

"Hayes!" he said urgently. "A horse behind."

"I been watching," snapped Hayes from above.

"They've already found us out," muttered Aristotle.

"Looks that way. No other reason for a lone rider to make fast time at three or so in the morning."

"He'll get ahead of us and warn them at Bunton's stop."

Hayes hawked and spat from above.

Mysteriously Creed slowed the teams into a quiet walk, and Aristotle wondered about it, suddenly suspicious of Hayes and Creed as well as this swallowtailed gambler beside him. A setup. They'd kill him. He peered back from the window again. Much closer now.

From above, Hayes whispered softly. "Figaro—recognize that buzzard?"

The gambler scrambled up and peered from the fore window. "I can't make him out."

Creed reined up the horses and the coach creaked to a halt.

"What're you stopping for?" cried Aristotle, sure now that he'd been betrayed.

Hayes's voice drifted down to him quietly, almost a whisper. "Ever try a long shot from a bouncing coach, Scrimshaw?"

Illumination came to Aristotle. He heard Hayes climb across the roof above him, and the tick of metal touching metal.

"Don't move around down there. Hold still," Hayes muttered.

"But you don't know he's an agent. He could be an innocent man, a miner escaping," Aristotle said. "We've got to stop him first and see."

From above, a low guffaw. Creed's.

The horseman closed behind, fifty yards, forty, then suddenly veered wide to the left, out upon the sagebrush flats that sloped into the gulch. At the edge of shotgun range.

"Son of a bitch," muttered Hayes from above. A horse coughed ahead and snorted.

The shattering explosion of Hayes's shotgun above jolted Aristotle. A second blast set his ears ringing. The lone rider's horse bucked violently, apparently hit by a ball. The dark rider spurred the plunging animal and raced ahead and out of range.

"You recognize him at all, Figaro?"

"Not really. Thought it might be Haze Lyons, but I couldn't tell."

Creed hawed the teams into a swift walk, and the coach rumbled and swayed again. A rider in front of them now. By the time they pulled into Bunton's Rattlesnake Ranch that afternoon, they'd likely meet a surprise party. All over before it got started, he thought dismally. Maybe they'd spare his life if he tossed them the gold. Somehow he'd get back to Annette and Margaret and Thompson, and start over—somehow. A bleakness settled through him. All his planning, his scheming, his daring, his calculation, his ingenuity. All his months of grueling cold labor scratching nuggets and flakes of gold from bitter gravel. All his hopes and dreams—all gone, along with his very life, probably.

Creed put the teams into a smart trot again, and Aristotle nursed his misery.

"We're dead before we start," he said to Randolph Figaro, testing the man.

"I'm a gambler," the man replied. "Wait until the last turn of the card."

Aristotle settled back in the bouncing coach, which banged his shins and tailbone viciously with every rock and pothole, his mood as black as the night outside. They sank into a muddy flat, and the coach wheels cracked through skim ice and mushed along through black muck. He felt the horses slow and tire as they dragged the coach through heavy road. Above, Creed and Hayes talked occasionally, muffled words drifting down to him, punctuated by rifle shots of cursing. From the tone of it, neither man sounded particularly worried. In fact, Creed sounded positively ecstatic, and his bull bellows thundered into the night now and then.

At the foot of Alder Gulch, near its confluence with the Stinking Water River, Creed pulled up. He clambered down and watered the sagebrush, while horses blew and snorted.

"Gallon of beer will do it every time," he bellowed.

Aristotle hopped out, shotgun in hand, suspicious of the stop and wondering if they'd be jumped here—if it had all been planned and these traveling companions were all road agent stooges. Why should he trust them?

"Scrimshaw. It's two, three hours to Daly's. Dawn's after seven now, and that's about right. If we're too early Cal'll slow up. We've got to find the fresh cayuses. You fetch and I'll hold a shotgun to the house. Big place, two story. We'll change again at Dempsey's and again at Bunton's Rattlesnake Ranch. Both by daylight. We should make Bannack City about evening, and the madam should be waiting somewhere around Peabody's express office. We'll load her after dark. That's when the fun begins."

"The fun?"

"Yeah. They'll wait and see what we do at Bannack, whether we load on anything more, and then hit us south of Bannack. Get it all instead of just yours."

"They'll hit us for sure?"

"You saw their rider go by."

"Can we trick them? Go only at night, hide by day?"

Calvin Creed tugged his gauntlets on. "Me and Hayes, we're full of tricks," he bragged. "Don't you worry your head, Scrimshaw. There ain't been an agent stopped me yet."

Creed set the team to a smart trot, and the night rolled by, so obscure Aristotle wondered how the driver knew where to go. They turned north, following the Stinking Water through open meadows and naked leafless cottonwood groves. Inside, Aristotle sweated even though the cold had grown bitter. Time stopped. He tried to doze but couldn't. He studied the silent gambler beside him, who did doze, or seemed to, in spite of the plunging of the seatless coach.

Gray light cracked the east behind them and the world turned foggy. They forded a creek and then another and crossed a long flat. Above, Creed and Hayes muttered to each other, and the horses slowed.

"Daly's ahead half a mile, gents," Creed bawled in a voice that would wake up butchered beef. "Scrimshaw. You get cayuses from the south pasture. A. J. Oliver's stock is in the north pasture and our stock's in the south."

In the slate light, they drew up before a silent log building with a splendid veranda. Daly's. Also known to some as Robber's Roost.

No one stirred. No one expected this coach.

Aristotle swung down and unhooked the lead team, stripping harness from it swiftly. With luck, he'd have the fresh horses harnessed in an hour. And by then they'd be found out, he thought dourly.

Chapter Nine

Aristotle could not escape the feeling that knowing eyes peered at him from every black window in Pete Daly's establishment. His senses had been honed keen by danger and desperation, so keen he felt, rather than saw, the razored gaze of others in the predawn gray. He walked warily out into the unfenced, tree-dotted bottoms looking for cayuses, a pair of halters in hand. Catching six spooky horses and harnessing them would be a long, tedious process, one usually completed by hostlers at each stop well in advance of incoming stagecoaches.

He dreaded leaving the sagging coach with his gold in it. He'd have to check the bags when he returned. He more or less trusted Hayes and Creed, but not the gambler, who could easily betray them with a drawn revolver anytime. But Figaro lay hidden in the coach, the jury-rigged canvas wall of the coach concealing him from Daly's log building.

No horses. Aristotle trudged through shadowed cottonwoods, through gnawed-down, naked pasture. No horses. Surely, he thought, they'd be out where grass grew better. For ten minutes he hiked through bottoms, while advancing light added color to the gray night world and the sky slowly blued. He struck taller grass, but still no horses. He'd walked the better part of a mile—far, far from his gold. Some sixth sense told him someone had been here very recently—a hint of dust in the air, perhaps, caught by his danger-honed senses. No horses. And time hemorrhaging. With advancing day he could see better, peer into distant groves and thickets, case meadows. He studied the long sweep of bottomland desperately, and knew he'd find nothing. Had they stripped the place of horses? Would the sagging coach pull out of Daly's with three spans of tired animals? He could wait no longer, and trotted back, fear caught in his throat. A trap? Would he find the others disarmed and his gold stolen?

As he approached Daly's log building, a sense of being studied by countless hidden eyes engulfed him. Whoever lurked in that long log building watched him with unblinking greed, knew him, knew of his fortune, and would murder him for it without a second thought.

Sweating even in the iced dawn, he hurried back.

Hayes's glance took him in.

"We'll try Dempsey's, over near Beaverhead Rock," Hayes said.

"They figured played-out horses will give them time to organize," Creed said. "I'll have to walk them. But we got tricks, right, Fortitude?"

"So've they," replied Hayes dourly.

"That rider that passed us?" asked Aristotle.

"That's about it. This coach's no secret now. They got us slowed down and they can hit us anytime, soon's they figure out who's aboard. They're probably arguing now, some wanting to get us soon, others wanting to wait until after Bannack City, see who else they can rob," Hayes said.

"Put the wheelers in the lead. Makes 'em think they're fresh," said Creed. "Actually, they ain't in bad shape. Three span and a light load so far."

Aristotle switched the spans, a simple matter, and fastened the breeching on the new wheelers.

"Let's get outa here, afore I blow some buckshot through Daly's genuine glass windows," bawled Creed as he clambered up to his perch.

Aristotle decided to join them up on top, and settled himself beside Fortitude Hayes, shotgun in hand.

The coach rattled out of Daly's yard, apparently wakening no one, but making noise enough to bring any stage station to humming life. From the high perch Aristotle felt the coach lumber and roll below him, smelled the acrid sweat of tired horses, and glared narrowly at every innocent copse of cottonwoods or brush. Creed's hands on the reins were as gentle and demanding and talkative as a lover's, and for a moment Aristotle admired the Jehu's genius. But he'd moved up to the driver's seat to deal with Creed, whose idiocy menaced them all.

"Good thing Figaro stayed hidden," he said for starters. "They think we're only three, not four."

From below, the gambler chuckled. "Ace up the sleeve," he said, his voice muffled.

"But now what? They're ahead of us."

"That rightly presents a problem," allowed Hayes.

"Nah. I'm gonna deposit this whole cargo at the Fort Hall stage station on the Overland, this and the Bannack City cargo, and any agents try to stop us, they're dead agents," bragged Creed.

The brag annoyed Aristotle. They might get through with planning and deception and sheer armed strength. But not on the brag of a bullheaded blowhard.

"Rather avoid a fight," Aristotle said. "People get hurt. Maybe you, Mr. Creed. Maybe we should hide, move by night, vanish by day, leave false signals, use our heads."

The driver bellowed nastily. "I captain this ship," he said.

It wasn't a reply but a declaration of command, Aristotle thought. Creed actually itched for war. Somehow he had to persuade this man to use brains as well as brawn, or they'd all die. As the coach clattered over the rocky two-rut trail, Aristotle considered simply abandoning it, pulling himself and his gold off at some hidden place, and leaving the bullheaded driver to his own devices. Cache the gold and strike out on foot. He glanced covertly at the huge driver, noting his thick-skulled aplomb, his smug stupidity, his plain arrogance.

The morning seemed deceptively quiet, cold and clear. At the ford of the Stinking Water, Creed let the team drink a bit, and then hawed the horses across and into the glistening sun-swept Beaverhead River valley, moist and still green, though the cottonwoods had turned golden or brown, and were half naked. Here the coach hissed through damp earth, slowing and tiring the jaded horses. Far ahead in the dawn mist lay Beaverhead Rock, or Point of Rocks some called it, and on this side of it, Dempsey's Ranch, the next station.

"Seems to me we ought to plan a bit before going into Dempsey's," Aristotle said quietly.

"That's still four hours off," Creed replied.

"Got to get fresh horses there," said Fortitude. "We can't lay that off no more."

"You'd be surprised what I can do with played-out horses," Creed retorted. "I'm hungry. You bring anything to eat?"

"Nary a bite," said Fortitude.

"Well, we'll stop at Dempsey's for eats. Jehus got to be hayed and grained."

Aristotle hadn't thought of food for a day, and Creed's needs surprised him. He didn't feel a bit hungry. The only tension in his belly came from terror.

"Takes time to grub an unexpected coach," said Hayes. "None of these stations is prepared for us."

"That's my point—we should be planning," snapped Aristotle. "Buy cold food. The more we delay, the more time they've got to get together a gang so big we haven't a chance. My whole idea when I started on this was surprise—never give them time to get organized—"

Creed guffawed.

"Scrimshaw, they're always organized. Part of them always on watch, ready to move," chided Fortitude patiently. "Surprise's gone now."

"What's left? Cunning—deception—or a fight," Scrimshaw replied. "I'm thinking to abandon the coach. Put the packsaddles on the team and walk out over the mountains."

"Leaving tracks any pilgrim or agent could follow," said Hayes. "And what about Angelica? You thinkin' only of your own precious self?"

"My idea to fix this old coach, the unscheduled trip," Aristotle cried hotly. "Maybe you should follow my plan!"

"Sure, and you were going to drive it, ride shotgun, and collect other armed men all by your lonesome," Hayes growled. But he cocked a head toward Creed. "Young man has a point. You rightly know what we're going to do? You rightly know how to get this Peabody and Caldwell customer and them other customers safe to the Overland Trail and the blessing of Ben Holladay's gigantic monopoly luxury line?"

Creed muttered and fashioned a reply, but it was bitten off by the sudden appearance of two riders ahead, dawdling out from a stand of cottonwoods. They sat their horses and appeared to be unarmed.

"This may be it," Hayes muttered. "Don't stop, Cal, and whip them up if . . ."

"Goddammit, Hayes," Creed growled.

Aristotle scarcely examined the two riders ahead. Instead he glared red-eyed at the brush, looking for the telltale glint of metal, or horses, or hats or men. He saw nothing. Ahead the riders sat their horses directly on the trail, intending to halt the stage. A good spot to do it, Aristotle thought. Marsh and cattails on the left of the road, brush shading back to trees on the other.

Calvin Creed's response was to cajole the horses into a trot and to mutter strange imprecations. He looked too happy.

Hayes's double-bored shot gun steadied relentlessly on the riders. Aristotle's weapon covered one flank, and he trusted the gambler inside the coach covered the other. From fifty yards, the riders looked nondescript, unshaven, dirty. Neither wore a mask.

"Anyone we know?" muttered Hayes.

"Casing us. Keep hidden down there, Figaro," Creed said.

"Whoa up!" cried the nearest rider. "We want a ride to Bannack City. Paid-up fare!"

"Not in service," Creed bellowed. "Outa the way."

The lead team closed to ten yards now, trotting briskly and showing no sign of slowing.

"Watch where you're going, dammit!" bellowed the other horseman. "Want to ride. We'll take roof seats."

Creed laughed, and peered down his long, curved beak at them from mean gray eyes. At the last moment the horsemen scattered, one into the cattails, cursing wildly, the other forcing his panicked horse into naked brush.

The coach hissed by, and Fortitude swiveled his scattergun rearward. Behind them, the riders returned to the road and stared dourly. In a moment, Aristotle knew, they'd race off with news for their colleagues.

"They like to do that. Slip one on board as a passenger. Makes it easy when the heist comes," muttered Fortitude. "They did it to me last week. Their ringer looked like a pilgrim."

Creed guffawed softly and slowed the teams, sending ephemeral signals down his lines.

"It's building up to something," Aristotle said shortly.

"They've got the advantage. They know about us. Where we're going. There's only one way to the Overland Trail or Salt Lake. They know our strength. Know we've got you and your gold aboard, Scrimshaw. It's up to them, and they'll hit us when they think they've the advantage," said Hayes.

"I'll be a surprise," said Figaro from the belly of the coach.

Aristotle fumed. "Can't we try a few things? Tactics? Strategy? Why leave everything to them?"

Calvin Creed answered, "You can't just take a stagecoach through wilderness. Got to be roads and stations to change teams, known fords at rivers. This was your idea, Scrimshaw, reviving this old coach. You have to play it out the way you started it. At

Daly's you got a lesson. They hid the horses. Now you know they can slow us and stop us at will."

"Why are you driving, then?" demanded Aristotle.

"Tickles me."

The horses settled into a steady walk, not yet showing weariness because three span were tugging a light load. Creed's canniness in moving the former wheelers to the lead team seemed to work. The horses seemed too dumb to know they had been used hard.

Ahead, Beaverhead Rock loomed larger, a prominent breadloaf of stone northwest of the verdant river bottom—and one of the road agents' favorite places to strike. Aristotle glared at the flat fields around him. He couldn't get these stagecoach people to think about anything: hiding the coach, detours, ambushing the road agents when they were waiting to ambush the coach, cunning, surprise. . . . Both Creed and Hayes seemed to think success lay in firepower. If the agents strike, whip the horses and start shooting. He wished he'd simply found some packhorses and slid out of Virginia City at night alone, rather than fixing up this fool's coach.

"You're upset, Scrimshaw," said Hayes, eyeing him sharply.

"We're sitting ducks, we're targets in a shooting gallery!"

Hayes said nothing. Then, "Why you want that gold so much? You ready to kill for it?"

The old sergeant knew him too well, he thought. The possibility of killing other mortals for the sake of gold had been crabbing at him, troubling him to his very marrow. And now the man beside him, the man who knew how to lead men into war, was probing.

"I hate the thought of killing anyone—even a murderous road agent. It comes so hard to me I'm not sure I could pull the trigger. I guess that's why I'd prefer to dodge and duck to get away, rather than get into a fight."

"I don't hear you saying you're afraid of death," said Hayes blandly.

"I'm afraid."

"But you don't want to live out your life knowing you've killed."

Hayes's probing disturbed him, and he evaded it. "The gold will help me just now. Foreclosing on my farm. My boy's a lunger, a consumptive, and I want to help—maybe a dry climate for him. My daughter's ill, last I heard. Maybe—maybe she didn't make it. My Annette, she's sinking into— I've got to get back and with enough to start over."

"Lots start over without gold."

"I grubbed for it! I was out grubbing in bad weather. I didn't spend it in saloons and hurdy-gurdies! I saved and bought claims and worked every day except the sabbath!"

Hayes hawked and spat, and a horse ahead lifted its tail. The beasts slowed now, as the weak sun climbed into crystal air.

"Two kinds, the workers and grubbers and doers who build, and the fighters like me, raise hell, tear it all apart. They don't hardly ever match up. Grubbers and farmers like you, you'd run from a fight if you could. Me, I'll fight. Makes my blood pound and my head wild, and if I live I got something to remember and a yardstick to measure myself. But I know your kind, Scrimshaw. Seen your kind in war often enough. Hard to get het up. Won't even pull the trigger on a man fixing to kill you—unless you get het up. But if a man like you gets himself cornered and mad and het up, God help your enemies."

Aristotle didn't much like being examined, and turned silent. The stage wove and leaned through a peaceful November morning, creaking and sagging.

"Figaro, you awake down there?" bawled Hayes.

"I'm asleep."

"You got treasure on you?"

Down inside the coach, Figaro paused. Then, "My winnings are in Dance's safe. I've got a small bank, mostly Mr. Lincoln's greenbacks—five hundred dollars, but trading at sixty cents—some dust, and two fresh decks of cards. That and a revolver, a hideout derringer, and a boot knife . . . and a locket and a tintype."

"Which of that is the treasure, Figaro?"
"None."
"You got scruples about fighting?"
"Men who've called me a cheat, or tried to kill me—they've died across the green baize. I have no feelings or scruples. Those things died in me long ago."
"They say you run a square game, Figaro."
"Not for ethical reasons."
"Why're you on this coach?"
"My hand is worth playing out."
"That why you're on the coach?"
"I confess to curiosity. Will our young colleague and his fortune outwit the agents? I'm in agreement with him, by the way. He wants to employ cunning, and escape. Brace the deck. It's more certain than a square game."
Creed guffawed.
At eleven they turned into Dempsey's Ranch and stage station, sagging somnolently in the sun.
"Dempsey's straight, we figure," muttered Hayes. "But the agents hang around here, and Dempsey keeps his mouth shut—to stay alive. He puts up a lot of hay for the company, raises truck for the mining camps."
Aristotle eyed the log place warily. No stage was expected at this hour, and he spotted no one. It irked him. They were driving into another dangerous stop without an iota of planning. They didn't scout out the place. They didn't check to see where the horses were. They made no plans—who'd cover, who'd shoot, who'd harness. Creed simply turned the weary horses into the lane. The horses turned eager, sensing the end of their ordeal, and trotted smartly toward the corrals and log barn.
"Stay low, Figaro," muttered Hayes.
No horses. Corrals empty. Distant fields barren. Maybe a trap. Aristotle's pulse built with each step of the horses. Hunger and weariness engulfed him. Cal Creed coaxed the team beyond the pens to the one-eyed log station emitting a thin coil of cook smoke. The coach stopped, creaking on its thoroughbraces.

Alkali dust curled up. Both swing horses lifted tails and dropped fresh green apples. A magpie leapt and flew off shrilling.

Aristotle squinted about red-eyed into the silence. Hayes spat, and Creed snorted. A shot broke the quiet, and the weathervane on the barn clanged. Blue steel shone from the dark barn door. Two men. Glass shattered, and a rifle poked from Dempsey's naked window. Fortitude roared and blew both barrels at the ones in the barn. Creed picked up his scattergun and blew shot into the window. They heard a yelp. Aristotle swung around to shoot, but a hard voice stopped him. Seven of them in the shadows, hard to pick out of the glare. Maybe more.

"Lay down the guns, you sons of bitches," sang a sandpaper voice from within the barn. "Lay them guns down or you're good and dead."

Hayes laid his scattergun down on the front boot, lifted another, and shot at the voice. Four blasts answered him, and bright blood blossomed along his neck. He jolted back, caught himself, and slowly eased his shotgun down.

"Pitch them guns off the coach," barked the voice.

Fortitude slipped into befuddlement, but Aristotle kicked a shotgun down, feeling bitter and full of self-righteousness. If they'd planned, cased the station, as he'd wanted, they'd have avoided this. And now he was as good as dead.

Chapter Ten

A skinny man with carrot hair and flapping ears stood before her.

"I have a message from the virgin," he said.

Angelica peered sharply around the gilded parlor and beckoned the man to her office. He followed uneasily, in an awkward shuffle.

"Never been in a fancy house before," he muttered, squinting purse-lipped at the lounging tarts and then at Angelica.

She closed the heavy plank door and lit a lamp. Acrid sulfur hung in the still air, and the amber light revealed the young man's nervousness.

"Your name?"

"Tim Harrell. I'm a hostler for Peabody and Caldwell, and they're letting me ride shotgun messenger now sometimes."

"You risk your life."

He nodded. "Fortitude says tomorrow afternoon, probably late. You're to be at the Peabody and Caldwell yards with your baggage. He can't bring the coach here. He hopes you have proper baggage."

"I do."

"He says it'll still be daylight and maybe you should stay hid. Might be a long wait if they get off late and all."

"*Dios*. Where will I hide?"

"Don't rightly know, ma'am."

"I've never seen you before."

"I'm fixing to become a preacher."

"Who'll be the others—the passengers?"

"I don't rightly know. In fact, I didn't hardly know this is about a trip or a coach. I can't figure it—we haven't got a coach leaving Bannack City tomorrow."

Angelica regretted saying and asking too much.

"*Mil gracias*—many thanks. I would offer you sport, but I suppose you . . ."

"Makes my pulse go. Specially that one with the big— I got to git," he said, backing awkwardly. He careened through the door and fled.

She smiled bitterly. The pain of her profession never left her, never eased her soul. She blessed herself with a sweeping sign of the cross. Ah, to leave here, to leave the terrible life! In the white city of San Francisco, the gentle Saint Francis, she would begin anew, quiet and respectable and far from the sporting districts. She trembled with the overwhelming vision of a life she could endure, pure and holy again. Confess and be made whole.

A message from the virgin. Tomorrow. In daylight. It all frightened her. In her armoire lay six valises, each with a hundred pounds of dust. Each too heavy for her to lift. How dependent she was on men. On Alfonso! And now on strangers, and Anglos, too, not a Catholic among them, probably! There remained one more thing, to pack her own valise first of all with the tintypes of her boys, and then a few precious things. . . .

Fear overtook her. Even if she got the gold safely to the Overland Stage station at Fort Hall, she still faced another thousand miles to San Francisco with a fortune in six valises too heavy for her to carry. Every hostler who picked up those bags en route would know instantly. Still, she might hire one of Holladay's coaches and an armed escort to carry her the entire distance—she had gold enough for that. Why was life so hard for a cast-out woman?

She summoned Alfonso, and took comfort in his huge brown bulk and the businesslike revolver holstered at his side.

"The time has come, Alfonso," she said. "I have the word. Be at the station through the afternoon tomorrow."

He nodded.

"I am to conceal myself if I can," she added. "How will we do that? I must not be seen waiting, and the valises must not be seen. There are always informers in the station. Bandits!"

The station lay almost a half mile distant, across Yankee Flats, on the edge of town and the road to Salt Lake City.

"Señora," he said. "You can't wait there with heavy bags and invite gossip. We'll load the wagon and you'll stay here and I will go loiter there until the time comes. Then I'll fetch you."

"Too much time! We must be there and ready, pronto, pronto!"

"But, Señora—they will not permit you."

Angelica sighed. A woman in the profession could not loiter there or in a nearby cafe. Not even one dressed soberly in black, as she always was.

"Señora, the sheriff keeps an office there. Ask him for permission. You'll be safe there, and the gold. And out of sight of the informers."

"Plummer? Henry Plummer? I don't trust him. He has cold eyes, Alfonso. Maybe he is honest. Maybe he is a bandit. But he has dead eyes. I see the dead eyes, and I shiver when his dead eyes look upon me."

"Señora, you have a better thought?"

No, she didn't. The sheriff occupied himself at the stage station, watching people come and go with contemplative eyes, doing business from his small log-walled room there. A polite man, yes. Civilized and courteous, with cold eyes.

"He'll know, Alfonso. He'll see the bags and see their weight as you carry them. If he's the wrong one to know, I've lost everything."

"No, Señora. Not everything. I will be there beside you to help load the bags. He's afraid of me. He's very fast, *verdad,* but I take much killing."

She could think of no alternative. In fact, she couldn't think at all. Anxiety knotted her stomach and was flowering into a headache that made her weak.

"Bueno," she said. He nodded and left.

She slept not at all that night, and paid no attention to business—Alfonso's business now. Instead she cloistered herself in her room, sometimes weeping with the tintypes of her boys before her, sometimes walking the confines like a caged animal, sometimes clutching the small, ornate crucifix and begging the mercy of Jesu Cristo. Once she said her rosary, muttering half forgotten decades, clutching wet, tear-soaked beads with trembling fingers, imploring the most merciful God to remember the wronged wife, not the woman in a desperate profession.

She remembered. The austere, pale man who took her to wife called womankind Sin. She submitted to lust, then his atonement of whip, lash, fist, and boot, and then long, passive coldnesses until lust consumed him again. It had grown worse over the years, madness in his eyes as he pounded her. . . .

By dawn, when her fancy house lay thick and quiet and the night's revelry had faded like old cologne, she felt calm and collected. And tired to her marrow. The looking glass revealed black pits surrounding fevered eyes and a face gone haggard. Not just from this, but from years of hard living.

Still, dawn of this last day in Bannack City crept over her peacefully enough. She had hours to kill until late afternoon. Sometime when the sun passed its apex, she and Alfonso would drive the spring wagon to the station and she would slide unobtrusively into the office of Sheriff Henry Plummer. She hoped he'd not be there. He would make conversation, eyeing her suavely, asking indirect questions, with eyes that would glance obliquely at her six valises and one larger portmanteau.

She peered out of her sole tiny window—glass was precious in this wilderness—across frost-rimed Yankee Flats and upon the cluster of log and board buildings. Gold made this town, she thought. Some had come here to find gold for good purposes, for the capital to begin businesses, buy farms. Others wanted gold to spend on drink and riotous times and—her mind blanked when she came to her life and business and the sense of shame she felt about it. Painfully, Angelica cheered herself. That life would cease! Her gold, her vast gold would bring her a new home, her past would vanish, she would find new friends, cherish the comforts of Mass each day, confess all this once and never again, begin new and clean . . . with the gold. Alfonso had been hard put to find the cowhide traveling bags, but eventually he bought four new and two used from pilgrims. Now they cradled her gold.

The morning ticked by like a cooling wood stove. Alfonso silently brought her tea, but she couldn't swallow and it grew cold beside her. She thought of her four girls, *putas,* sleeping through the quiet hours. They came and went. Some she despised. Others, like bright Clarissa, she adored and invited to her rooms for tea and the comforts of sisterhood. They'd still be sleeping when she left, most of them. She thought to slip into each room, hug each one—she was experiencing a great melting of heart, a flood of uncharacteristic emotion, she thought—and then wrestled the thought aside. The fewer who knew, the better. Alfonso would be good with them. Strong and gentle and tolerant. But the poor soiled doves—*Madre,* how would they like working for a man, an *hombre*? Still . . . Clarissa. One quick good-bye and a kiss for sleepy Clarissa.

Alfonso appeared. "Señora, the sun goes toward the ridge. The spring wagon is ready and the mule harnessed."

She stood, peered around her, and found tears welling. Maybe she should forget the gold and just go, go, go. She, a hard woman, crying. Tears from granite, tears leaking from steel and oak! Peddler of flesh and lust gone soft.

"Alfonso," she whispered. "*Bueno*. You are good. You are my Alfonso, and I love you much."

The giant's black eyes went soft. "It's been good," he said.

"And now you flee to a new life. It's good, and the new day is bright. Count on me."

Angelica dabbed at her eyes with a lacy handkerchief and watched Alfonso lift two heavy valises at a time, as if they were filled with cotton. Outside, the spring wagon creaked under the mounting load. She slid down a gloomy, narrow hall that smelled of old perfumes and more sinister things, and opened a creaking door. Clarissa stared.

"Madam?" she said, sensing something.

"I am saying *adiós*, Clarissa."

"You're going?"

She nodded. "A new life. Alfonso is a good man and you'll be happy."

It took the girl a moment to absorb that. Then, "Good-bye, Angelica. You treated me good. If he does, too, I'll stay. I got treated bad—in Denver City. Beat up and cheated and drugged to make me stay. A whore ain't got much except hope to earn something and get out. I have fun sometimes, but mostly—rotten men. You let me keep my dust. If he treats me bad—"

"*Dios!* How I know!"

"I won't ask where you're going."

"No, don't ask." Angelica sat beside the reclining girl and kissed her cheek gently. *"Adiós,"* she said, and stood. She didn't look back.

The day glared. The blue wagon creaked as she settled into its padded seat. She stared resolutely ahead, not looking back at the somber, silent building humped darkly on the outcast edge of Bannack. Alfonso drove directly to the coach yards and the scatter of pole fences surrounding the weathered log station, a humbler place than Jack Oliver's competing coach and express company office in the heart of Bannack. Sheriff Plummer had an office there, too—in fact, spent more time there than here. Travelers fascinated him.

No coach was expected this cold afternoon, and the yards lay somnolent, unattended. Her heart lifted. Perhaps she could sit quietly in an obscure corner—the sheriff's digs were never locked. If he had secrets, he kept them elsewhere. She paused, reading the schedule, a white flyer pasted to a plank beside the entrance. Triweekly service, Concord coaches, express and regular, to Virginia City or points south: Beaverhead, Red Rock, Camas Creek, Eagle Rock, Blackfoot, Fort Hall, Portneuf, Brigham City, Ogden, Salt Lake City. Connections with Overland Stage at the Adobes station, Fort Hall. Through service to San Francisco and points west; Kansas City and points east.

But not today. Relieved, she stepped inside the gloomy station redolent with the smell of horse, tobacco, old cigars, and human sweat. A crude place, packed earth floor, whitewashed windowless walls. Plank benches to sit on. A crude counter across the west third of the room, and behind it battered luggage and a few crates with waybills tacked to them. And on the east side, a door cut through logs and a lean-to room beyond . . . and muffled voices. She sagged.

Sheriff Plummer materialized in the door, and behind him his deputy Charley Forbes. Plummer, excellently dressed as always in a black broadcloth wool suit, newly pressed, and immaculate white shirt with a fresh boiled and starched collar, swept his dead gaze over her and seemed unsurprised. Behind him, the rough lantern-jawed deputy peered with apparent disinterest.

She wore her best—and most funereal—suit, also of black, and a small silver crucifix on a chain over her bosom. Plummer's eyes focused on that, and the faintest surprise showed in them.

"Madam Ramirez," he said. "I'm surprised. There are no coaches today."

Dios! What to say to this man who was already probing. She trembled, suddenly afraid.

"Ah . . . Mr. Plummer. I've come to meet a friend. Yes, I have come to wait for a friend."

Plummer started to say something and bit it off. Instead he bowed politely. "Why, wait in my office with me, señora. I've just been discussing things with Deputy Forbes. The road agents, you know. I hear they pulled some miners off a coach a few days ago. Surely it's a poor time to travel. I hope you're not traveling."

She didn't dare answer. Outside, Alfonso waited in the spring wagon with six valises filled with six hundred pounds of gold dust and nuggets.

"No. I—I will sit here. No. I'll go back and come later. I'm early. My friend—isn't coming yet."

She felt utterly rattled, and turned to leave. But Alfonso stood at the door, a valise in each thick hand. The sheriff's glance slid across the valises and settled on the burly man's revolver.

"Why, I see you are traveling, Madam Angelica. Salt Lake perhaps? A little vacation? Alfonso, put madam's luggage in my office. She can wait there."

"But—this is the wrong day! I thought the coach was coming today! *Dios!* I've made a mistake!" she cried, her voice sounding strange to her, trapped in her soft throat.

"Deputy, help Alfonso with the bags," the sheriff said blandly. Before Angelica could protest, Forbes stalked out to the spring wagon and lifted two valises.

"I'll be damned," he muttered, hefting astounding weight. Plummer's eyes rebuked him coldly. Angelica saw that. This sheriff and this deputy were blandly pretending not to know what they knew, and it frightened her.

Plummer sensed her fear and responded. "You've come to the right place," he said gently. "It's my job, my office, to protect you. You should have let me know earlier, and I could have arranged protection. I've got to send Deputy Forbes out on patrol, but I'll personally stay here and guard you. Why, madam, I wish you all happiness and success in your new life."

She nodded shakily. Forbes and Alfonso settled the last valises and her portmanteau inside Plummer's office.

"Is Alfonso going with you?" Plummer asked amiably.

She shook her head, too afraid to talk.

"It's good that he's here with you. A woman needs the protection of a good man, eh?"

Alfonso settled himself beside her on the bench inside Plummer's office.

"Charley, I'm staying here to guard Mrs. Ramirez and her possessions while she awaits her connections. You take over for me in town, and of course keep this matter entirely quiet. We wouldn't want careless gossip to reach the ears of the roughs around here."

"Sure enough, Henry. Anything I should tell your missus?"

"Only that I may be late."

Forbes left, and Plummer settled easily into a creaking straight-backed chair behind his plank desk, the only chair.

"You've acted wisely, making your private arrangements, madam. The trails are more dangerous than ever."

His eyes probed her softly and his voice seemed mild, too mild. She didn't trust him. She'd heard rumors. He grew too fat, lived too high on a sheriff's salary. Why, the dust he squandered in her fancy house alone was many times his salary. . . .

"You are very kind to wait here, Sheriff, but it's not necessary. I have Alfonso, and he is *muy* . . . very strong."

"I wouldn't think of abandoning you, Angelica. Will you make the connection soon?"

Always probing, she thought. "It may be a long time," she said. "You will want to attend to your business."

He smiled. "This is my business. I suppose you are leaving us? Have you sold your place—or am I trespassing on your private matters?"

She smiled. "A long trip," she said. It was odd. She could evade, but she couldn't lie. *Dios!* She'd wanted from life only to be a pious, faithful wife of a Santa Fe don, honorable in all ways, with little to confess to the padres . . . and now what was she? A retiring whoremonger. But perhaps she might not lie. She would make careful words.

"I hope you return," he continued suavely, cleaning dirt from his nails with a silver pick. "Bannack's a growing place, a fine place. Quartz gold next, after the placers run out. . . . I hope you've chosen your traveling companions carefully. I hear the road agents have informers everywhere. They tell me Peabody and Caldwell's riddled with them at every station."

"Yes," she said shortly.

"It's odd," the sheriff mused. "No coach today. The company doesn't even have spare coaches. Everything's in service. You'll be using Peabody equipment, I suppose. You've done well here, and I trust you'll have armed men you trust. I have my suspicions about some of them. Perhaps I can warn you. . . ."

She nodded, revealing nothing.

"I trust you're armed, madam. Not that a woman should use weapons or risk being shot. But a small derringer or handgun is a comfort. And sometimes it is helpful."

She nodded. In fact, she had more than a little hideout gun. She had a deadly pepperbox and a five-bore .32-caliber revolver and knew how to use them expertly. Long ago she'd decided a woman running a fancy house had better know how to defend herself and her girls. She'd never had to use the weapons—not with the faithful Alfonso keeping her out of harm's way—but she didn't doubt that she could shoot to kill, as coldly as she had to.

Beside her, Alfonso grew restless as the minutes ticked by. She understood. The house he had acquired lay rudderless, no one at the helm, and he itched to go back, tell his girls, prepare for the night. . . .

The November sun dipped behind the high ridge to the west, casting the gulch into cold blue shadow. Somehow a tormented afternoon had twisted by. Sheriff Plummer sat amiably, lighting an occasional small cigar, gazing at her with kind, calculating dead eyes, glancing at the seven dwarfs at her feet, pausing at the small silver cross on her black bosom. And still no one came. No coach, no connection. Hayes didn't make it.

At last, as twilight settled, she made up her mind. "Alfonso," she said. "No one comes. We will go back. I will stay."

Plummer smiled. "I'll stay on," he said. "If anyone comes, why, I'll fetch you, madam." He rose from behind his desk. "Here, I'll help Alfonso load your baggage."

She watched distrustfully as Plummer started to pick up two valises and dropped them.

"Good lord," he exclaimed. "You're carrying a lot of weight, Angelica."

Chapter Eleven

From a gap edging the canvas wall of the coach, Randolph Figaro watched masked men emerge cautiously from sheds and the barn door. Six of them, plus the one whose rifle still poked through the broken window of Dempsey's station. He didn't recognize any. Some simply wore bandanas and low-crowned felt hats. One or two wore Harvest Queen flour sacks with jagged eyeholes over their heads. Small fry, crooked hostlers and informants. The important road agents had roistered away the night back at Churchill's.

So he would die after all. He hadn't escaped. This robbery in a stage station itself tempted fate. High stakes. They knew that, and acted on it. He felt oddly collected and cold, not even tired after the exhausting night. He'd become a slave of Lady Luck, and if she spun out the two of clubs now, that's how it would be. He slid his small .32-caliber revolver from its shoulder holster and the hideout derringer from his pocket.

Above him he heard Hayes muttering and cursing. Figaro gathered the old sergeant had been grazed. Creed and young Scrimshaw apparently were stanching a wound and helping him.

"I said git your hands high," yelled the nearest of the road agents at Creed and Scrimshaw.

"We got an injured man," retorted Creed testily.

"Forget him and get down."

Above, neither man moved.

Two of the robbers rounded the back of the coach. Three others approached from the canvas-covered side. The sixth stood behind with a shotgun at the ready.

Not the slightest tremor of flesh or palpitation of heart disturbed Randolph Figaro as probably his last seconds on earth ticked out.

Both men had black beards poking below their bandanas, and grimy felt hats. They closed upon the coach door, their eyes opaque with visions of loot. Randolph Figaro shot one in the heart and the other through the mouth. They sagged, grunting and dead, into the dust, leaking bright blood.

The coach exploded under him, spoiling his aim at the third one who bolted toward the coach. Wildly Creed cursed and hawed the tired team and it bulled ahead, faster than the men behind could run.

Behind, a shotgun boomed and pellets ripped the canvas wall, missing him, leaving sun dapples. A second blast had no effect.

"Stay low!" Creed bellowed to Scrimshaw above. "Don't shoot back; just keep the coach between us and them!"

Figaro wondered how long this would last. Played-out horses. Apparently they still had a shotgun left up there on the driver's seat. He eased his revolver into the gap between the canvas wall and the coach frame, spotted a running bandit, and shot. He missed, but the man stopped running.

"You all right, Figaro?" yelled Creed over the rattle of trace chains and wheels and trotting horses. "They botched it," he added.

"They'll catch up in a moment," the gambler replied. "Then, sir, the hand will play out the way it was dealt."

"You're a fatalist," yelled Hayes. The voice startled him.

"I thought they got you."

"They did. I'm leaking from a neck muscle."

"They'll finish it in a minute," Figaro said.

Creed laughed shortly. "Buncha amateurs, all bunched around the rear of the coach. None of that outfit ever robbed a coach before. The small fry of the road agents. All I done was whup up the horses!"

"Quit braggin' on it and tell me how much is left in the horses," Hayes snarled.

In response, Figaro felt the coach slow as the driver pulled the weary animals to a walk.

"I can get miles outa them yet," Creed bragged.

"They know I'm in here now," said Figaro to the unseen men above him. "The hand plays out."

"I don't know how you ever survived as a cardshark," snarled Fortitude Hayes.

"By rote."

Scrimshaw said, "I have a shotgun, Figaro has some handguns, and you two have sidearms. We'd better be thinking how to get shotguns. They'll come after us on horseback."

"You think too much, Scrimshaw," said Hayes. "War is mostly surprises and improvising."

"If we'd planned we wouldn't have gotten ambushed!" Scrimshaw raged. "It's my gold you're playing with!"

Creed snorted condescendingly, but from within the coach Randolph Figaro again felt the young man had a point.

They rolled below the looming escarpment of Beaverhead Rock and on up the flat open valley of the Beaverhead River. Ambush would be unlikely here, the gambler thought; they could see in every direction for miles now that they had passed the landmark rock. And they could spot horsemen trying to circle ahead.

He felt faintly amazed at his coolness during the attempt on the coach. Had fatalism infected him so much? Didn't he care about living? The thought triggered another, and the image on the locket and tintype came to him briefly. The bullet intended for Amanda's lover killed Amanda, too. He'd been a young man then, devoting too much time to his accounts and not enough to her, though he loved her madly. She had died in Figaro's arms, naked, bloody, choking, gasping, angry, sobbing, and unforgiving. Her parents didn't forgive either, and hounded him with the law. The riverboats became his floating homes, and he slipped from one to another, sometimes staying in his small cabin when he spotted a passenger he knew. He'd been a master at poker; he had only to add the faro layout. Now suddenly in this fool's coach facing death, he wanted to start over, give up the green baize tables, and live out his days quietly in the shipping business once again. The need came keen to him, like an epiphany in that bouncing coach, and clashed sharply with the fatalism that had permeated his soul.

Up on the driver's seat, they were exclaiming about something. A coach ahead coming at them, he gathered.

"There's our nags," bellowed Creed.

"It's one of Jack Oliver's coaches," muttered Hayes.

"I'll borrow them nags anyway."

Hayes snorted. "That's what I like about you, Creed."

The gambler felt the coach roll to a stop. He eased his bruised body from the pile of saddlebags he sat on, and stepped down to earth, watching the other coach slow up. The Oliver coach had no shotgun messenger, only a wiry, dark driver with a vast, ferocious black mustache that concealed his upper lip.

"Mornin,' Jackson," said Creed.

The Oliver driver peered warily at Creed and the rest on the bench up there, and then settled on Figaro.

"Thought that coach of yourn had died and gone to hell," he said.

"We're fixing to borrow your teams and give you these. Played out, but they'll walk you to Dempsey's. We just got held up there."

"Right in the station?" Jackson rolled a chaw around his brown-lipped mouth and spat. "What you got in this wreck besides tinhorn gamblers?"

"Gold," roared Creed. Scrimshaw winced. Figaro simply

gripped the small revolver that now rested in his suit-coat pocket. He had no view of who rode in the Oliver coach.

"They get you?" asked Jackson thoughtfully.

"Got me," muttered Hayes.

"Idiots were all bunched behind the coach so I drove off," Creed bragged.

The dust-caked horses that Creed had coaxed these last few miles sagged in their harnesses, heads low. Jackson eyed them skeptically.

"How far they come?" he asked.

"All the way from Virginia."

"I'll lend you my leaders but not the wheelers. That should git you to Rattlesnake Ranch. Don't know why I'm doing it."

"I don't either. You must be dumb, Jackson," bawled Creed.

Heads peered out of the windows of the Oliver coach now. Drummers, a sporting man, a matron.

"Are we going to be held up by agents at the next station?" asked a drummer.

"Could be," Jackson said. "They pick on salesmen." He clambered down and unhooked his lead span and Scrimshaw did the same. In a moment Creed had some reasonably fresh animals that would get him to Bunton's place.

Fortitude Hayes slowly climbed down. "I'm going to nap in the coach," he muttered. "Neck hurts me some. Figaro, you want my company or do you want to sit up there?"

"I'll let Mr. Scrimshaw ride shotgun," he replied. "I have a yen to sit on his gold inside."

"I think they're waiting for you at Bunton's," said Jackson. "A dozen extry men lollygagging around there when we rode in."

"Entertainment," said Creed. "Word got ahead of us."

"Gold does that," retorted Jackson. He flipped his lines and the Oliver coach rattled off, its passengers staring.

"Well, gambler, let's you and me guard Scrimshaw's gold," said Hayes, swinging into the coach. Figaro followed and settled himself on the hard floor, facing forward.

The blood at Hayes's wound had coagulated brown, and the old sergeant seemed to ignore it. Beneath them, the coach lurched and then creaked slowly ahead. A few vagrant flies buzzed around the coach and then flew out the open windows into cold sun.

Something had delayed Lady Luck, the gambler thought. But she'd settle her score soon enough. Maybe on the hock card. Across from him, Hayes swayed limply and drifted into sleep. Figaro didn't sleep. He sat and stared wearily, wondering why he felt nothing, nothing at all, after taking the lives of two robbers. He wanted to make peace with Amanda's parents if he could, but now a civil war raged between them and him. Too late anyway, he supposed. He'd taken six lives now, and the sporting life had transformed him.

They forded the Beaverhead River a few miles upstream and walked the tired horses slowly toward Rattlesnake Ranch, the next stop. Creed had Scrimshaw put the fresher horses in the wheel position and the played-out animals forward, and then they toiled up the gentle grade out of the river valley and into the dry foothills that heralded the approach to Bannack City. No one harassed them through the somnolent, chill afternoon.

Sitting on the driver's seat, Aristotle glared at the pacific world around him, and occasionally at Creed beside him. The bull-headed driver was plainly going to take the coach right into Bunton's, just as he drove into Dempsey's, without plan, without caring, almost begging for trouble. Aristotle glanced covertly at the man, at the flashy shirt and neckerchief, at the studded belt and fur-lined gauntlets and rakishly set hat, and at the formidable nose that seemed to plow the world like the knife-edge of a clipper ship prow, dividing and humbling everything in its path.

"Why don't we wait until dark to go in?" Aristotle asked. "We can get in and out safer in the dark."

"You afraid or something?"

"I don't want to borrow trouble. That's my gold in there. I scratched and wrestled it. I clawed it out when everyone else huddled around fires and stoves. I need it now—my family's in a bad way."

For an answer, Creed squirted brown tobacco juice to the side of the lumbering coach. More and more, Aristotle despised the man and dreaded Creed's knuckleheaded way of doing things.

"In the dark, I'll get the horses together and lead them to someplace this side of the station, out of their sight. We can change teams a half mile this side, and just bypass that place."

Creed coaxed the weary animals through a muddy flat that sucked at the wheels. A swing horse stumbled.

"Done in," muttered Creed. "I'm going to cut him out. He'll drag the others now."

The driver stopped the stage and waited. The battered coach swayed almost imperceptibly in the gusts of northern air.

"What are you waiting for?" asked Aristotle.

"You cut that off-side swing horse. Just cut him loose and throw the harness into the boot in back." With that, he swung down and began to wet a sagebrush.

Arrogant Jehu! Raging, Aristotle clambered to earth and unbuckled the harness of the exhausted animal. He pulled the bit from its mouth and dumped the bridle and long lines in the boot, along with the rest. The horse acted too tired to walk, so Aristotle slapped it and it stumbled out into the sage-dotted slope, too weary even to nip the cured dun grasses there.

Angrily Aristotle started to clamber to his seat again, but Creed stayed him.

"You ain't done yet. You got to put that single horse in the lead, and the lead team at swing."

From the seat, Creed watched, occasionally barking orders while Aristotle fumed. But at last the remaining five horses were harnessed in proper order, and Aristotle resumed his place on the padded leather seat. He took up the shotgun and felt the coach bite at his tailbone once again.

"They'll either have the horses hid or have them ready for us," Creed said. "They know we're a-coming; know we'll want cayuses. If they've hid the horses, you aren't gonna find them by prowling at night. If they've got the horses ready for us, it means they got other plans."

Aristotle felt too irked to respond. He'd discovered he felt starved and thirsty, too. He hadn't eaten since the day before.

"You got any better idea, Scrimshaw?" goaded Creed. "You got fresh horses stashed somewhere?"

Aristotle no longer had anything to say. He'd come to regret the whole fool's business, repairing this wreck, enlisting help. He should have just quietly slipped out of Virginia with some packhorses, stayed off the trails, cut right over mountains until he reached safety. He cursed himself for his folly. Still, here he was, alive, with strong men, his gold with him, and the wheels of this vehicle marking the miles. What worth had the gold? As much as his life?

He had no answer to all that. If the question had been posed in a church, he'd have nodded at the preacher and agreed, yes, riches weren't worth all that—life, love, health, the comforts of friendship were all worth more. But he wasn't sitting in a church, wasn't listening to some soft-fleshed preacher. Some hard anger keened through him, making his trigger finger itchy and his temper raw. Tension laced with hunger tightened through him and he felt mean and ready as Bunton's hardscrabble cluster of gray shacks and pens hove into sight, set in a crease in barren dun slopes a long, desolate distance from anywhere safe and sociable.

Slowly Creed steered the team into the yards and halted. Unlike Dempsey's stop, men lounged everywhere here. Some sat on corral rails, feet tucked behind the lower rail. Others leaned on porch posts. Rough, dirty men eyeing the unscheduled coach familiarly, as if the news of it had preceded it.

From within the coach rose Figaro's guarded voice: "About half of these were in Churchill's last night," he whispered. "They came around us somehow. I see Whiskey Bill, Buck Stinson, Haze Lyons . . . and there's Parish and Gallagher. Cooper there. Carter . . . Zachary. Ned Ray at the pens."

Aristotle glared at them all, ready to kill. Here they lounged, the very ones all the whispering had been about. The ones who'd killed scores of men—no one knew how many—along the trails for gold, for spite, for anything. He clenched the shotgun, some wild thing ready to explode in him.

But nothing happened. These rough, bearded men grinned easily, kept their sidearms in their holsters, and stared amiably.

"Creed!" said one. "Didn't expect no coach at this hour. The company fix up that old wreck, did it?"

"Taking it to Salt Lake for a rebuild," Creed bawled. "You got some horses ready?"

In fact, they did, six of them, all harnessed, waiting patiently in the pens. Two hostlers ambled out and unhooked the five stumbling animals, ignoring Aristotle's bloodshot, fierce glare and the black bores of his shotgun.

Creed clambered down and stretched. But neither Hayes nor the gambler stirred inside the coach.

"You got some chow? I'm plumb starved," bawled Creed.

"Lotsa chow," said someone wearing a star.

"Well if it ain't Charley Forbes," said Creed. "How come you're not over to Bannack making the rounds?"

"Sheriff's plumb worried about road agents, so he's got me out scouting," Forbes replied. Rough men laughed. "I don't suppose agents would hit a beat-up outfit like that, coming through on no schedule. No passengers. It ain't worth the trouble, I'd figure."

"I don't suppose so either, Charley," Creed replied.

Efficiently the hostlers hooked the fresh, newly brushed horses to the coach, attaching tugs to doubletrees, ignoring Aristotle's feverish eye and shotgun.

"Who's the fellow riding shotgun, Calvin?"

"That's Scrimshaw of Virginia City."

Aristotle shrank at the naming. Was there anyone in all of the mining district who didn't know of his fortune?

"I'm gonna get me a sack of grub and eat it on the road," Creed said, ambling into the weathered log station. "Come on in, Scrimshaw. We got the law protectin' company property."

Forbes laughed amiably.

"Thought you was a miner," said one of the hostlers to Aristotle.

"Jack of all trades," Aristotle muttered. "And master of none."

He decided to wait at the coach. If they intended to steal his gold, he'd kill a few of them first. He just couldn't bring himself to walk even a few yards from four hundred pounds of dust in a station yard full of road agents. But beneath him the brown-enameled coach quaked, and Hayes and Figaro stepped out.

"Well, if it ain't the professor," exclaimed Zachary. "You out taking the air, Figaro?"

"Vacation," Figaro replied coldly. "Actually, a dalliance."

They chortled at that. A dalliance.

"What happened to your neck, Hayes?"

"Mosquito bit me," muttered the sergeant acidly.

Aristotle sat rooted to his seat while his companions disappeared in the station. Was it a setup? Would they kill him now, when he and his gold were alone? Was it all planned this way? He felt his body grow still and taut while he waited for the barrage of lead that would topple him from his perch. But it didn't come, and below him, grinning men ignored his red-eyed glare.

Some infinity later when the shadows lay long on the gray clay, Creed, Hayes, and Figaro emerged, fed and rested.

"I'll ride shotgun, Scrimshaw. I feel right refreshed with that haunch of beef and them beans in me. Here, I brung you some Salt Lake City cheese. You git down in there and rest."

Reluctantly Aristotle stepped down and settled himself in the bowel of the coach again, Figaro across from him. Above, he heard Creed haw the team, and felt the coach lurch ahead as the fresh horses stepped out smartly.

"Why? Why didn't they jump us, Figaro?" he asked.

"Who knows?" the gambler replied. "Maybe the pot isn't big enough yet."

Chapter Twelve

Bannack looked meaner, Aristotle thought as the camp hove into sight far below in the lavender twilight. Obscure amber light glowed from a few windows in the log buildings. Beside him, Creed eased his team down the twisting grade, masterfully guiding the battered coach toward its destination, the Peabody and Caldwell station on the far side of town.

The arrival of an unscheduled coach from Virginia City didn't attract attention—such an event happened often enough. It was the dinner hour and few people dallied in the cold streets to watch a battered old coach with a canvas tarpaulin forming one of its sides rattle over the rutted road. No one would rob it here, but Aristotle eyed passersby and shadowed alleys dourly, swinging the shotgun toward perceived danger like a compass needle toward magnetic north.

A quieter town now than when he'd left, he thought. He'd worked a claim upstream from here for several months, getting good color from mediocre digs through hard work, patience, and care, before joining the rush to Alder Gulch. Bannack hadn't died. In fact, it had started to switch to hard-rock mining, wrestling gold from quartz veins.

Hoofbeats and the rattle of wheels and trace chains echoed from darkened buildings in the gulch as the coach rolled toward Yankee Flats. Creed straightened, tilted his hat, tugged at his gauntlets, kept his team in a smart trot, and stared back at passersby with the sublime assurance of his high station in life. For once, the glowering Aristotle felt amused.

They thundered over planks bridging Grasshopper Creek, and slowed up at a dowdy stage yard with a sagging station that looked to be thrown up with a day's labor and then ignored totally. An enameled blue spring wagon attached to a single dray loomed before the dark station. A woman sat in it; a swarthy giant was lifting valises into it. At the door of the darkened station a man in a dark suit lounged, his boiled white shirt popping out of the dark in startling contrast to the gloom around him.

"The sheriff," said Creed easily. "Don't know why Plummer's here for an unscheduled run, but he makes it his business to meet all the coaches, Jack Oliver's and ours."

"And the ones in the wagon?"

From within the coach Fortitude's rasping voice: "That's our passenger and her man. Don't rightly know why Alfonso's loading valises rather than unloading."

"Plummer. Wouldn't you know," said Figaro from down below. "Wouldn't you know."

Aristotle had heard the whispers about Plummer. The man in the fine broadcloth suit lounging so casually in the murky dark could well be the chief of the road agents. No one dared say it aloud, at least not so baldly. But it hunkered there. The man's sudden wealth. The company he kept. The deputies he'd chosen. His failure to bring even one of the road agents to book. His frequent sudden disappearances, always, he claimed, to have a look at prospective silver properties in the district. That and the men who'd died by his swift, deadly gun, rivals mostly, under strange circumstances that never quite seemed proper.

The stage slid to a halt, and Aristotle felt the coach body sway forward on the thoroughbraces and sag down. Dourly he swung his shotgun around, not quite at the sheriff but close enough. The short woman and the giant beside her at the wagon stared. So this was the madam. Another lowlife. He'd never seen one before, but anyone in her profession could not possibly be honest. Now he'd have to watch her as well as the gambler, he thought irritably. It made him wonder about Hayes, recruiting people like this.

"Evening, ladies and gents," boomed Calvin Creed. "Extra coach here for them that's traveling."

"It's you, Creed," said Plummer, but his eyes had focused on Scrimshaw, gently surveying the young man and his shotgun. For a moment their eyes locked. "Well, Madam Ramirez, your coach has finally arrived."

He smiled amiably, revealing even white teeth in the dusk. "I think you'll have some pretty fancy protection against those road agents," he added, as Hayes emerged from within. The intact side of the coach faced Plummer and the darkened station. Aristotle peered down, expecting Figaro to emerge, too, but the gambler elected to remain in the blackened bowel of the coach.

"*Dios,* Señor Hayes. We'd given up," whispered Angelica. Behind her, Alfonso stood guard over the valises, not yet willing to transfer the fortune to this shabby coach.

The woman waited for something, quietly surveying Creed and then Scrimshaw with a tension that was more felt than seen in the indigo twilight.

"Angelica, up there is Aristotle Scrimshaw. And Calvin Creed. A couple of tough men who'll look after you," said Fortitude.

She said nothing, studying them with her large brown eyes, trying to discern character. At last she nodded. The approval irked Aristotle. Her approving him!

"Scrimshaw," said Hayes. "You got to round us up some fresh horses. Creed here don't do it because Jehus don't do it, and my bum leg won't let me."

Aristotle felt annoyed, but handed the shotgun to Calvin Creed and clambered down. He hated to leave his gold. Especially with

Plummer there. The man might be honest, but who could tell? It struck him that Hayes had said nothing about Professor Figaro huddled on the floor of the dark coach below window level, out of Plummer's sight.

The woman watched him observantly, and finally shrugged and nodded to her man, who began toting heavy valises to the coach.

"You fetch them over, Alfonso, and I'll slide them in," said Hayes in a voice that brooked no dissent.

He's covering the professor, Aristotle thought. Which meant that Hayes didn't trust Plummer any more than he did.

Reluctantly Aristotle unhooked the road-worn horses, span by span, and led them to a pen where he slid harness off. This would take time, he thought. A half hour if he was lucky. It grew dark. He'd be finding fresh horses, no doubt skittery around strangers, in full dark.

Behind him a match blazed and the sheriff fired a cheroot, light raking his face for a moment.

Aristotle grabbed two bridles and trudged out into a pasture looking for the fresh stock, edging farther and farther from his gold. It turned out to be a large paddock with scarcely a blade of grass in it, and on its far side a shadowed mass of horses stood, restlessly aware of his measured tread. It occurred to him these might be unrested horses from an earlier run. He couldn't tell and it couldn't be helped. They spread edgily as he approached, swinging just out of range.

Fool's coach. When he'd planned the whole thing, he'd scarcely given a thought to replenishing horses. At stage stations fresh horses usually stood harnessed and ready as a coach rolled in, and he'd hardly realized that some hostler had expected the coach on schedule and rounded them up and harnessed them beforehand. Delay, delay . . .

He caught one just as it jerked its head up, and slipped the bit between its teeth. With one in hand it became easier for him to snatch the second. He took them back to the pen and found Fortitude ready to harness them. The sergeant set to work, saying nothing. Aristotle caught the second pair, and then the third, and both men harnessed quietly in the blackness, doing the job out of long familiarity.

They did the last horses together, Hayes at his side.

"Plummer tried to get a peek in the wagon but didn't quite dare mosey that close," said Hayes in a voice so low it scarcely drifted beyond Aristotle. "Wanted to see what—and who—was in there. Maybe curiosity, maybe more than that."

"Did he see?"

"Don't think so. I swung those valises in, and Figaro hunched out of sight along the front wall. I warned Angelica—that's the lady—I warned her not to be surprised; no seats in there."

"She's in the coach?"

"No. She's gabbing with Plummer. Alfonso, he got the drift and sort of set himself between Plummer and the coach windows."

"We're going to get hit—now they got her gold and mine to go after," muttered Aristotle. "And that crook saw it go in."

"Don't know for sure he's a crook. Greedy, yas," replied Hayes. "We'll get out of town and have us a leetle talk."

"We're down to one shotgun," said Aristotle dourly.

"That reminds me—got more locked in the comp'ny office. Also got to get Angelica to pay her fare."

They led the harnessed horses back to the coach, hooked the wheelers to their singletrees and hung the wagon tongue between them. A moment later the coach lay ready, a poised monster ready to bolt into the night.

"Madam," said Fortitude, "if you'll just step here into the Peabody offices—we got some settlin' to do with the comp'ny."

Plummer followed them amiably, his dead eye alert as Hayes struck a lucifer and lit the lamp on the counter. The whole transaction took place under the sheriff's watchful gaze, and in the end, Aristotle knew, the sheriff had a good idea of where Angelica was going—Fort Hall and the Overland Trail—and how much weight she carried—six hundred pounds, in Hayes's carelessly rounded figures.

Hayes locked the dust in the company strongbox and pulled two more shotguns and cartridges from the rack behind the counter, while Henry Plummer watched blandly. Hayes grinned and pulled a Sharps rifle from the rack, too.

"Leetle longer range than these scatterguns," he said roughly to Plummer. "Them agents respect a Sharps. Knock a buffalo down at four hundred yards."

Plummer smiled. "Good idea," he said. "But I doubt the road agents would hit a coach they know nothing about. It's always dangerous, but you'll be as safe as any that tried to get away from the camps. Good luck to you. I wish I had the manpower to escort you out."

Hayes turned down the lamp and they walked out into the chill, starlit night.

"Now, madam," warned Hayes. "Don't you be surprised by nothing in there. No seats. You'll be sitting on them valises and it's going to be a rough trip."

She smiled gently in the night, and turned to Alfonso.

"*Vaya con Dios,* Alfonso. It is strange I say that, yes. The woman with the *putas* saying that. But *vaya con Dios. . . .*"

She hugged the giant man, and Aristotle spotted a wet gleam on her ivory cheeks. A madam leaking tears.

Then Hayes helped her into the black coach.

"Dios!" she exclaimed as the coach rocked. "You got baggage everywhere," she added in a voice a shade too loud.

"Scrimshaw, you get inside with her. I'm gonna ride shotgun this first leg," said Hayes. The sergeant handed him a shotgun and clambered to the top of the coach, stepping on the small near-side wheel to pull himself up.

Plummer started to amble to the coach, but Creed hawed the team even before the startled Hayes got seated.

"Creed, you goddamn idjit," bawled Hayes against the hooting of the Jehu.

"Dios," muttered Angelica. "And who—Señor Who Hides—are you that I sat upon?"

Behind them, Sheriff Henry Plummer sucked his cheroot until

it glowed white in the night, and Aristotle saw a shower of sparks whirl into the night wind.

"Madam Ramirez, I'm Randolph Figaro, a sporting man. They call me professor."

"The same from Bannack City?"

"Correct."

"The same from Churchill's in Virginia," she said tartly. "I think maybe this is not right." She dug into her reticule in the dark. "If you move or signal, I'll kill you."

Something glinted blue in her hand as starlight caught it.

"And you, too, señor," she said to Aristotle. "This pepperbox, it kill you both very fast with many shots. This is bad, *malo*. I should not have trusted Señor Hayes."

All this she whispered so quietly that the driver and messenger above would not hear it. Aristotle sank into quiet, feeling the bores of the pepperbox upon him and Figaro. Nerve-racking, he thought, grasping for something to say.

"Madam, between us is four hundred pounds of my own—"

"Quiet," she hissed. "I will not listen. If you talk, I'll shoot you. What is a poor woman to do to protect herself?"

Aristotle listened to the coach creak and rattle through the night. A fat yellow moon squatted on the eastern horizon, turning the night gold.

Beside him, Figaro moved stealthily, hand sliding into the pocket of his coat. The man probably had a revolver in hand.

"Madam, your caution is admirable," muttered Figaro.

"Silencio!"

"I barely escaped Churchill's with my life," he continued, ignoring her.

For an answer she lifted the pepperbox and pointed the six bores into his face.

"Pull your hand from your pocket slowly and hand me the revolver there," she commanded. "*Poco a poco* or you are dead."

A tic in Figaro's face spasmed.

"Madam—" began Aristotle.

A stiletto whirled out of nowhere, slicing the back of Aristotle's hand. He winced and felt blood ooze.

"We're in this together!" he cried and ducked as her hand darted out again with its deadly silver tip.

"What's a poor woman to do?" she hissed. "I will die first!"

"Scrimshaw, what's up?" yelled Fortitude from above.

The woman swung her pepperbox into Aristotle's face, and he dared not answer.

He heard muttering from up on the driver's seat, and the coach slowed and then halted, creaking in the night breeze. Someone clambered down and swung the coach door open violently. Her shot exploded deafeningly within the coach.

"Goddamn," snarled Hayes, who had thrown himself sideways. "Angelica—you get the hell out here and put that thing down."

"I knew it! I knew it! What's a poor woman to do? I'll kill you first," she cried. "Take my *oro*—my gold. Take my life. I knew it!"

Aristotle sprang over the heaped bags of gold, clamping one massive hand over her stiletto-wielding one and deflecting the pepperbox with the other. It exploded, driving a second shot through the coach roof.

"I knew it!" she screamed, and bit his arm savagely. He felt teeth lacerate flesh and sharp, fiery pain.

Figaro sprang across the bags, and in moments they subdued the screaming, sobbing woman, who continued to writhe under their combined weight.

Fortitude Hayes collected the pepperbox and the knife, and roughly patted the writhing woman, finding a second dagger strapped to her calf.

"Let her out," he said quietly. Aristotle felt more like bashing her, but he released her slowly, expecting trouble. The gambler slid aside. Angelica Ramirez lay shaking, sobbing, coughing, as hostile now as before, but disarmed.

"Kill me now!" she cried. "Take the gold. I'm not a *puta* and maybe *Dios—*" She coughed and shuddered, her small, wide body convulsing within her rumpled black suit. Fortitude reached in and drew her bodily out into the cool night air.

"Kill me!" she cried. "I knew this. I knew this to happen!"

The old sergeant didn't speak, but settled into the grass near her, waiting. Aristotle stepped out into the night, seeing the bowl of heaven above him, sniffing fresh sagebrush. A horse snorted and shifted in its traces.

"Aristotle, pull out a saddlebag and show her your dust," Hayes said.

"My dust is riveted in."

He shrugged. "Professor, make your case now."

"I dealt at Churchill's but I didn't join them. They decided to recruit me or kill me, madam. I'm fleeing for my life. I have nothing with me—not even the faro layout with which to make a living. Some greenbacks, dust, and cards."

"Kill me pronto. Take my gold. I'm tired," said Angelica. "I am only an abused wife, and I try hard to survive after— No good, no good. Let me say one Our Father and I will be ready."

"Angelica, damn your ornery hide!" roared Fortitude.

She peered at him with pained and resigned submission. "It is always so for a woman," she muttered.

Professor Figaro rummaged in a breast pocket and pulled two small objects out of it. A locket of some sort and tintype. He handed them both to Angelica.

"What is this? Why do you do this?" she asked wearily.

"The miniature is of my wife. The tintype my parents. She's dead—by my own hand. In all the world, these two things are all I care about. These, and a memory of love, madam."

"Why do you show me this?"

He shrugged, not answering, and retrieved the things that were so precious to him.

She stared. "You took the treasure of the heart that was important when you escaped from Señor Churchill's."

Aristotle slipped into the coach and pulled out one of his heavy saddlebags, dragging it over to the madam.

"Is there something in the boot to tear it open, Fortitude? I'll show her my dust."

"Chisel and mallet," said the messenger, swinging toward the rear boot.

Angelica stopped him. "No, don't. It is true, what's in his bag. I see how heavy it is."

"I think we'd better show you," retorted Aristotle dourly.

She glared back at him and then walked disdainfully into the bushes while they stood waiting. When she returned, her face had softened and he thought he detected pain and remorse in those soft brown eyes. But no tears.

"Let us go, then," she said.

"Not so fast," said Creed from his seat. "We got every road agent they can git together stalking us now. You just set a minute and think how we'll get through to Red Rock. That's the next station, at the river crossing. Also a favorite hangout of theirs."

It was that, thought Aristotle. A cottonwooded flat not far from where the Bannack City road joined the one to Virginia City. A strategic place commanding both trails.

Hayes peered thoughtfully into the night. "They'll likely go all out for this one. Fell trees, barricade. We won't be able to run for it. You got bright ideas, Cal?"

"Sure," said the driver. "We'll go around."

Fortitude Hayes laughed skeptically. "No way around," he said. "The mountains will dump us into Red Rock near the station."

Creed looked miffed. "This Jehu can take a coach through the eye of a needle."

"And silently as an owl glides," Fortitude retorted.

"It's one or the other?" asked Aristotle.

"Those are the choices, Scrimshaw."

"We'll take the road," said Fortitude Hayes. "The other—going overland—that's crazy. We'd end up hung up in a gulch or busting an axle or tongue. We don't even have a shovel to make road or clear paths. And you can't hide the backtrail, six horses and four iron tires. You can't make a coach disappear for long.

It's the road. We'll stop and scout ahead whenever we hit a likely spot. There'll be no surprises."

No one disputed him. He spat, eyeing the old brown coach. "A thing or two we can do now," he said. "That canvas wall blinds you in there. Gimme a knife."

He cut two U-shaped flaps in the canvas, both low, one forward and one rear.

"Now you got some holes to see through, shoot through, and down low, too, where you can lie on the floor and fire. Now help me move these bags around."

When the old sergeant had finished, valises lined the sides and rear of the interior, forming barriers against flying lead.

"You lay low on the floor and you got good protection. Might as well put all that gold to good use," he said.

It looked good to Aristotle. The three passengers would lie on the buffalo robes spread on the coach floor, surrounded by bags.

"One more thing," said Hayes sharply. "This ain't robbery we're facing. It's robbery and murder. For half a ton of gold, they'll kill every witness. Don't think for an instant they'll grab the gold and let us go. You—Angelica—you understand that? We get through or we die."

She nodded.

"We can go back. We can drive you to Bannack and drop off anyone that doesn't want to risk that—the dying. Hole up in madam's place, safe and sound."

No one said anything.

Chapter Thirteen

Professor Figaro lifted the flap of canvas with the barrel of a shotgun and surveyed the moonlit world outside. Steep, barren hills, silvery in pale light. On the other side of the coach, young Scrimshaw sat bolt upright on a valise and stared out the window. Between them the madam swayed on a buffalo robe to the coach's rhythm.

They were climbing, the professor thought. The Jehu kept the animals to a steady walk, keeping them fresh as the coach toiled along a curling road that followed ridges and shoulders of barren hills. Not a good ambush place. Not yet. But neither Creed nor Hayes were talking up on the driver's seat.

"I'm not ready for death," said Figaro to no one in particular. "I wasn't ready at Churchill's and I'm not ready now."

No one replied for a moment.

"This is a fool's coach," muttered Aristotle. "My idea, but I didn't think it through very well. My stupidity is risking your lives—and mine."

"We're here by choice," the professor replied.

"I became greedy. *Dios,* the gold owns me. Bad gold, from sin. If I die, it is right."

"I understand you're trying to put your . . . profession behind you, madam. Surely you are too hard on yourself."

"I could do that—I could walk away without gold. But I am taking sin-gold. I will die for it."

"Walk away without money? Into what?" Professor Figaro persisted.

She didn't answer. A wheel hit a rock ledge and the coach lurched. He suspected the thump carried half a mile into the quiet night. That and the subdued jingle of trace chains and clopping hooves and the creak and rattle of an iron-wheeled coach.

"If I die, I will take a road agent, maybe two, into hell with me," she said. "They will think about shooting a woman, and while they think I will shoot."

Scrimshaw looked as if he wanted to say something, but he wrestled it back from his lips. Then he muttered. "It's too late, too late."

"What's too late?"

"Too late for life. I could have left without my gold. Gone back to Wisconsin and my Annette and had life."

Figaro laughed shortly. "Those road agents—they've been killing people who carried nothing. Shot them out of spite because there was nothing to steal. Especially you. They'd have killed you for the sheer pleasure of it, Scrimshaw, just because you mucked out so much dust."

"I know," he said. "I'm a fool."

"Not me," said Angelica. "They would not kill a woman, not even one like me, if I'd simply taken a coach and left. I could have gone safely away. I am a fool, yes?"

"We'll see."

"You—Señor Scrimshaw. You are here in the district from the beginning, and you never set foot in my place. You muck and work and save. You are faithful to your Annette. You are thinking of her and never having a good time, never having release. Never drinking and playing. God should favor you.

God should take you and your gold past death and robbers."

Scrimshaw sighed. "It doesn't pay to think that way," he said. "What you see as virtue I see as my own greed. But it's no good to brood. We should be thinking what to do when we're hit."

"You can't escape God," she said tartly. "He comes after you. He's going to make me dead now."

She annoyed Figaro. "Madam, if your God is so cruel, why do you believe in him? I take it that you are running toward him, and not away from him, at this moment. Does he love you or doesn't he?"

"It's the gold," she said.

The professor poked the flap open with the barrel again, and peered into the moon-silvered night. They had climbed almost to the divide that lay between the Grasshopper drainage and Horse Prairie. Ahead the ghostly road swung into a long, blind uphill curve, running alongside a gulch on the left and a ravine on the right. He felt the coach slow and halt.

"Scrimshaw," said Hayes from above. "We got to scout this next one. I'd do it but for my bad pin. Git outa there, and I'll show you a stalking trick or two."

The young man eased out the coach door and into the night. Figaro heard them consulting out there, and watched the young man slide wraithlike up the angle of a hill. A fool's mission, he thought. The agents would be watching Scrimshaw's every step, and would gun him down.

Hayes must have been thinking the same thing. "Creed, this goddamn moon of yours is like to get the lad killed."

"Try driving without one," the Jehu retorted.

"He is good," said Angelica. "The young man. He deserves better."

Randolph laughed shortly. "Virtue is no passport to anything. I am a fatalist. From soda to hock, the cards fall as they will, and some will live and some will die."

"You had love once," she said. "Was she a good woman?"

"I found her in bed with another man."

"So? So. Was she a good woman?"

"Yes. I had ignored her."

"I never had love. My marriage was arranged. I took into my bed a man whose soul was cold, *frío,* very cold. He did not love. But I had virtue once, and maybe a little bit left now. It is all I have left to please myself. Not once did I sell myself. But I'll die anyway, *sí*?"

"Maybe we'll have a winning hand."

He watched a ghostly figure wend down the long, silent slope and approach the coach, rifle in hand.

"Nothing," said Scrimshaw, and eased back into the bowel of the coach. Creed snapped the lines and muttered something, and the Concord rolled lazily forward into the arching night.

"Nothing down in there," Scrimshaw repeated. "They've had time to gather an army and get ahead of us. When it comes, it'll be fifteen or twenty, and from all sides, and with some kind of barrier thrown up to keep us from running. This isn't going to work, scouting the bad places."

Hayes heard him. "You got better ideas, Scrimshaw?" he called down.

"Not yet," yelled Aristotle. "But I'm thinking."

In his mind's eye, Professor Figaro could see the shape of the future. At some clock-tick ahead, the night would explode. Fifteen or twenty blasts from shotguns, rifles, and revolvers. A hail of lead right through the coach. Driver and shotgun messenger hit at once. Hayes would probably unloose one shot before dying. Four or five horses would be downed in the first volley. The coach would drag to a halt. There'd be a brief flurry of shots until Scrimshaw and he were meat. One or two more shots when they pumped bullets into Angelica.

They topped the divide, and Creed halted to let the team blow.

"Creed," said the professor, "it's flat or downhill all the way to Red Rock, isn't it?"

"Mostly downhill."

"You don't need six horses. Four will do."

Creed didn't answer.

"I'd like to take one and scout ahead," said the professor.

"Fast way to get killed," snapped Fortitude.

"The rest of you have better reasons to live. Especially Mr. Scrimshaw."

"I'll not stay behind trapped in a coach," Aristotle retorted. "If you go, I go."

"You have everything to lose, Mr. Scrimshaw. Think of Annette, and your son and daughter. I have less to lose."

"You can ride one flank and I'll ride the other. Between us we're safer than if you go alone."

"Get the hell back in the coach," snarled Creed. "You jaspers don't know how to stay on a bareback horse."

But Professor Figaro ignored him. He'd ridden bareback enough as a boy, and he thought Scrimshaw, the farmer, would have no trouble. He unhooked the leaders while Creed fumed, and threw the harness in the rear boot, all except for the bridle and long lines. Beside him, Scrimshaw was doing the same thing. The gambler stepped up on the front wheel and slid onto the horse's back and joined Scrimshaw.

"All right, all right," muttered Fortitude. "Listen to an old sergeant. Stay in sight of each other and watch each other constantly. You hit trouble, they start shooting, you wheel and run back here. That's all we can ask—not to be surprised. No heroics, no shooting it out with twenty agents, and you skylined on a horse. You get back here and maybe we can fort up, all of us together. Goddamn, I wish I could go with you, but this weak pin—if I fall off, I'm done for. Don't be heroes. They'll kill the first hero they see."

"I'd be obliged if you don't shoot us when we come in," replied Scrimshaw mildly.

"One more thing. You leave those long guns here. You got no way to stow them on bareback nags, and no slings. You got revolvers, but not for using. You're going out there in them gulches to reconnoiter, not start a fight. You get that?"

Figaro thought that Hayes sounded like a clucking old hen, scolding tenderly.

"Señor Hayes, maybe they go away to tell the agents we're coming."

"Angelica!" roared Fortitude. "I'm going to stuff a bandana in your mouth if you keep that up."

Randolph Figaro felt the thin, hard backbone of the nag cut into his crotch as he kicked the horse ahead. Beside him Aristotle rode silently and with greater ease.

"You prefer any side?"

"I'll take the right, and stay two or three hundred yards from the road and a mile ahead of the coach."

"That's pretty far from me. When the moon sets, we'd better stay closer."

They angled apart at a trot, the professor to the left and the miner to the right, gaining ground on the lumbering coach. In a few minutes the sound of the coach vanished altogether and the gambler found himself riding across a silent barrens, with a few copses of pine and some juniper on the slopes. He would sacrifice his life, he knew. He hated dying. He had utterly no wish to cash in. Each birthday was like a fresh bankroll to wager. Each day was like a deck of cards to play out. To live was to enjoy a fortune. But for reasons he couldn't fathom, he'd volunteered to do this thing, ride into the gates of hell. So that others might be warned and live? No, nothing so generous as that, he thought. He didn't have a martyr's toenail in him. Curiosity, he decided. He wanted to see how the card fell when he'd bet the whole bank.

Angelica Ramirez sprawled on a dirty buffalo robe, thinking about the holy sacrament of matrimony. The robe did nothing to insulate her small body from the jolting of the coach, and the constant hammering had bruised her flesh and made her irritable. She lay alone; the belly of the coach was all hers now, with those *hombres* scouting ahead.

She remembered the wedding. The bishop himself presided, adorned in lace, giving the blessing of Holy Mother Church upon the union of Don Santiago Ramirez and Angelica Cruz. If seemed all good and right. God himself smiled, Jesu Cristo and the Virgin and the angels all smiled, and as the Latin Mass progressed she felt most comfortable about the middle-aged man beside her, Don Santiago, who had arranged with her father to share her life with her. She'd glanced shyly at him through her veil, noting the thin hawk's nose and gaunt, ascetic face of the man, and thought she might learn to love him. That night, on the marital bed, all thought of that had vanished, and by dawn her purple-bruised body tormented her so much she wished to leave it.

The mystery had remained. All this was good and blessed by the Church. Upon hearing her tearful confessions, Father Alonso had tut-tutted her, and told her she must repent and learn to live in Christian harmony with Don Santiago. And so she did, year by year, powdering over her bruises, cloistering herself many days when her body bore signs of his cruelty, wondering how God and the Church could proclaim all this to be good and sublime.

She'd fled Santa Fe with nothing. With less even than the gambler Figaro, she thought. She barely realized it, but by the time she fled she lacked spiritual furnishings as well, for she'd found no comfort in the Church or its cold male priests, no succor from above, though she'd wept and prayed.

Now as she rolled and bounced in the black belly of the Concord, she suddenly hated her gold. The wages of sin. Not just the Church, but the whole world proclaimed it to be so. She'd poured dust from countless pokes onto scales, weighed out a *puta*'s wage and returned the poke. Half was hers, and after house expenses, she still had a quarter as pure profit. These things the *putas* did in their cribs with men, behind doors and curtains, these things were mostly accepted by the Church when done in holy matrimony, but blackest evil when done outside of it, and for gold. Her own experience of matrimony lay so darkly upon her that the memory festered as raw as her wounds, but the Church had pronounced it good. On the other hand, her *putas* sometimes had good times—mostly they did. Once in a while a bad time, a bad *hombre*. But always the world condemned them, condemned her, and called it evil. It all made her head ache.

Mostly her girls joked and lived high, and Angelica had talked endlessly with them about it, pried and probed, because she had never held a gentle lover in her arms and it mystified her that some men could be thoughtful and kind. In the end she'd built up a mental wall and refused to think about such confusing things as good or evil. She'd devoted herself to the real and practical, shut up the spiritual, and lived out her days collecting gold dust, recruiting new girls to replace the ones who so constantly eloped, and learned even to laugh sardonically at the itinerant preachers who blew into Bannack, condemned her, and held up marriage as the sacred ideal.

But now on the hard floor of the coach, surrounded by a fortune won from women who sold their loins and hands and mouths, she suddenly hated her gold. A loathing of it exploded in her, as unexpected as darkness at noon, oppressing her and crushing her chest. Astonished, she raised herself up to peer at the fat black valises, and saw nothing unusual about them. Nothing sinful. Nothing evil.

"Madre de Dios," she said aloud.

Her invocation of the Virgin comforted her. The woman in heaven. Surely the woman would understand the lot of women. Especially women of the Church. She imagined the Virgin smiled at her, comforted her.

Tears welled. The first tears in more years than she could remember. They collected hotly in her eyes, scalding them, wetting her ivory cheeks. Sin-gold. For years she had planned this escape, and now she knew the sin-gold would kill her. She would never see her boys again. Never see the sun again. Never smell lilacs or watch grass bend with the breeze. Never live out her days in quiet respectability in a distant city. . . .

She lay sobbing softly, sobbing away the last moments of a desperate life, suddenly sorry she had done what she had done, sorry she had run a parlor house, found girls, taken gold. She should have killed herself, only that was sin, too. She should have run away—that would only be a small sin, not one so large, so impossible. But what could a woman do?

She felt the coach roll over the barest of roads through a wilderness scarcely explored, taking her toward hell. Her tears slowed at last, and a cold calm replaced the hot, choked convulsions of her body. Around her lay the valises, squatting black and sinister, heavy as dead souls. She loathed them, loathed the leprous pigskin and cowhide they were made of, loathed the hundred pounds of sin that lurked within. She had to throw them out! Get rid of sin-gold, and then she might live! Go naked to the Church, to God, to the confessionals of the cold priests—go naked with no gold and only a repentant heart, and then she might live!

She stood up in the swaying coach, bracing herself as best she could, glimpsing the whitewashed world edge by outside. She tugged at one black valise and couldn't lift it. The hundred pounds would be more than she could handle. And yet . . . with a mighty jerk she dragged it a few inches. And a few inches more. Toward the door. Panting, she rested. A lurch of the coach tumbled her, and she lay despairing a moment, feeling fresh bruises. Sin-gold. She would give it to God, give every ounce away, and then she might live. The road agents wouldn't kill her because she had no gold. *Nada* . . . Jesu Cristo wouldn't condemn her because she had no gold. The Virgin would smile and protect her because she had no gold. *Nada*. . . .

She opened the coach door and it clattered back.

"You open that door, madam?" asked Hayes from above.

"Only a moment. *Momentito*."

"Not a good idea, Angelica."

The door banged again, and she tugged a valise enough to wedge it open a way. He might not stop her. He sat on the far side, but the driver, Creed, might look down and stop her. Trembling, she worked across the rumbling coach and found another valise and yanked it fiercely. It didn't move, snared by a cleat that had once anchored a seat. Sobbing, she yanked fiercely, and this time she scraped the heavy bag over and gained a foot. Then a second foot. Exhausted, heart tripping, she yanked it farther, closer to the door. At last she dragged it to the lip of the floor, where she could pitch it out.

"Bueno," she said, knowing she had five more bags full of sin-

gold to pitch. She shoved, lost her balance, and nearly careened out herself.

"Madam," snapped Creed. "What're you doin' down there? You want I should stop for a moment? Need some privacy? That door ain't supposed to be flapping like that." He started to rein in the teams.

"No, no, don't stop. I am—I will—" she cried.

From the open door she peered back across frosted slopes, whitened by a high moon. Three horsemen, pale riders, shadowed messengers from hell, in the blurred distance where moonlight faded. Three horsemen of the apocalypse.

The shotgun messenger saw them, too.

"Three behind us," he hissed to Creed. "Comp'ny coming at last. And them amateur scouts of ours forward and no help a-tall."

Fear froze Angelica.

"Get that door closed, ma'am, and lie low behind them valises," said Fortitude Hayes quietly.

"Dios!" she cried, desperately tugging back the valise she'd used to prop open the coach door. "I am too late. Now I will spend all eternity in the bottom of hell."

Chapter Fourteen

The three pursuers stayed carefully out of rifle range.

"Speed up a little, Cal," said Fortitude. "I want to see if they stick."

The Jehu hawed the horses, and they broke into a smart trot across the flats of Horse Prairie. Fortitude squinted back—the light was bad—and watched. The horsemen stayed glued to the trail, just out of range of the big Sharps.

"Slow her down, Cal," he said, and watched the pursuers slow down, too, keeping a respectful distance.

He spat. "They're tailing us, all right, Cal," he said. "And they seem to know I've got the Sharps. Interestin', huh? Not shotgun range. Rifle range."

"Plummer," said Creed.

"They're following to keep us from turning around and hightailing it to Bannack when the trap springs," Fortitude said. "They ain't strong enough to attack themselves, but they got rifles enough to shoot horses and hang us up. Sort of Plummer's insurance policy. Like Injuns pushing buffler toward the buffler jump."

The shotgun messenger mulled the meaning of it. In a moment they'd reach the edge of Horse Prairie and plunge into twisting gulches again, to Horse Prairie Creek, and then follow the creek-bed on down to Red Rock station. Instinctively he felt that trouble would strike at the station and not before. There'd be plenty of good ambush places along the gulches and twists of the creek, but there wasn't any wood around to make barriers, and a coach getting through, getting past them, might get to Red Rock station, get fresh horses, and get shut of them. No . . . they'd tie up old Hospers, the square-enough geezer who ran the place, and jump the coach right there at horse-changing time.

He squinted into the bright, high-domed night again. Somewhere ahead his two scouts rode, down in the creek gulch now. He peered behind and saw the horsemen measuring their pace to the progress of the coach.

"Cal, when we start into the creek bottoms we'll go down a long blind double curve. If I recollect, there's a gulch coming in. Want you to turn up that gulch and whoa up. I'm gonna see if I can surprise those buzzards and fetch us some horses."

"You figuring on taking on three?"

"Two barrels, each with nine double-aught shot. Ain't a sane highway robber that don't pay attention to that."

"You'll need someone with good legs to tie 'em up, if you don't plan on ticketing them to hell."

"Rather not shoot. Noise might echo clear down to Red Rock."

"Take them five minutes to untie themselves."

"That's all right. I'll have the horses and their guns."

For ten minutes more, they rode across frosty flats, and then Creed steered the creaking coach into the head of a coulee and down a soft grade that twisted and turned.

"Speed up a little," Fortitude said.

"Hard on the horses downhill," said Creed, pushing them into a rough trot as the coach jarred and heaved behind.

"There it is. Pull in there and swing it around," Hayes said.

Creed swung the horses sharply leftward, off the rutted road and behind a steep headland. The coach careened over rough ground and then sagged as the Jehu halted the animals and wound the lines tight around the broken brake lever.

"*Dios!* It is the end!" cried Angelica.

Hayes climbed down swiftly and peered into the coach.

"No, madam, we're just going to hold up the holdup. Now don't you go shooting folks running around here."

He and Creed trotted straight to the point where the road circled the shoulder of land. Nothing grew there to conceal them, but they'd take their chances. His leg hurt as he limped his way over stony prairie, but they made it in time, Creed hunkering in the shadow of the boulder on the far side of the ruts, and Hayes simply flattening himself in a cold trough of dry clay.

Behind them a horse blew and snorted. They waited quietly through taut minutes, wondering if they'd been found out. They hadn't. Three horsemen materialized above, two on dark horses, one on a dun or gray—no way to tell which—and clopped deliberately down the long grade, sometimes out of sight, hidden by curves. Conversation drifted with them, but Hayes couldn't make it out.

"Don't git overeager, Cal," he whispered. "Let me call the tune."

Across the way, Cal nodded irritably. The man hated instruction.

Fortitude had been in battle and close to death a hundred times, and always his pulse drummed at the terror of it, and now as the road agents approached—fifty yards, thirty, twenty—he felt his usual giddy wildness. Ten yards, and Hayes sprang up.

"Hands up, you sons of bitches!" he roared, using the exact words employed by the agents at their dirty work.

Three shadowy men, faces shaded by wide-brimmed sombreros, peered around wildly. Two saw Hayes, glanced at the shotgun, and reluctantly lifted arms. The other spurred the dun horse, yelled, and grabbed for his revolver. Creed's shotgun exploded;

the rider screamed and tumbled slowly, his foot caught in a stirrup as the bloodied horse bucked and bellowed and trotted a few yards.

"Jesus," muttered a road agent.

"Slow now, unbuckle them belts and drop them down," snapped Hayes. "You ain't slow and easy, you're dead."

Hayes squinted alertly, but these two weren't going to tangle with a scattergun at twenty feet. The belts slid to the clay with a soft thud.

"Git down," he said, "and turn your backs to me."

"You fixing to shoot us, Hayes? Gonna let us write a letter home first?"

The voice seemed familiar. "Down," he said. "Slow. You lay a hand to those saddle carbines and you're dead. Cal, go poke that other one and watch out if he's up to tricks."

The Jehu edged cautiously to the bloodied road agent sprawled awkwardly on the grass while Fortitude watched two men, both short and lean, ease off their mounts.

"Don't hold them reins either, gents. You let go of them horses," he said, waggling the barrel of his shotgun at them.

They stood with their backs to him.

"Slowly now, reach down and lift your britches. I want to see them boots of yourn."

No hideout guns. Maybe a knife or two still, but he'd deal with that later.

"Turn around and pull off them sombreros," he said.

They did.

"Well, if it ain't Marshland and Zachary. Thought you gents looked familiar."

"We were just heading on to Red Rock for a party, Hayes. You got no right—"

Fortitude hawked and spat.

Creed returned. "Other's dead. That dun's ringy, got shot in his croup."

"Who was he?" Hayes demanded.

"You killed him? You killed him!" yelled Steve Marshland.

"That's about what you fellows do to travelers, Marshland."

"I'm innocent! We're innocent."

"Party at Red Rock. About what I figured," muttered Hayes. "Lie down, you two."

"You can't kill us! My friends will hunt you down—"

"Down."

Fearfully the pair settled to earth, their gaze glued to the bores of the shotgun.

"You can't!" Zachary snarled.

"Roll over. On your bellies. Hands behind you."

"You got anything to tie with, Fortitude?" asked Creed.

"Reins from that dun horse, if you can get it."

With that and lines and thong scavenged from the boot of the stage, they trussed the road agents.

"You're cutting off the blood, that's so tight, dammit! You gonna send someone to free us?" cried Marshland.

"Not if they kill us afore we can talk."

From downstream a soft voice carried. "Hayes! Creed! We're coming in."

Fortitude straightened up and peered sharply, satisfied that the approaching horsemen were his own people.

Moments later Professor Figaro and Aristotle Scrimshaw sat their horses, gazing at the trussed road agents, the dead one, a bloodied and crazed dun, and two saddle horses.

"Now, Steve, you should have coppered that bet," said Randolph Figaro. "Good evening, Bob. Last I knew, you were sitting at my layout."

Zachary spat.

"Who's he?" said Randolph, gesturing at the dead one. "I don't recollect meeting him at Churchill's."

"He's got family in Bannack City, and that's all you need to know. Six-gun family," snarled Marshland.

"Time to get along, gents," said Fortitude. "I'd admire for you to harness them draft horses again, and then take them two saddle broncs and fit your fannies to them."

"We rode clear down to where there's a view of the Red Rock

Valley and the station, and there's nothing between here and there," Aristotle said. "But we make out that station as a likely place."

"All right. It'll be Red Rock station," said Fortitude. "Now when you get done harnessing, I want you to get aboard them new cayuses we got and follow along behind, just like these crooks here were doing, outa rifle range. One thing. See them kerchiefs around their neck, both knotted the same? You put them on. I seen them too much on that bunch and it figures to be some sort of sign to them—that way you'll look to be one of their bunch, at least in the moonlight. One other thing. Tie that dun horse behind the coach if you can fetch it. I don't want these hog-tied fellers to get notions."

"We'll kill you! Top of the list, Hayes," Marshland snarled.

A few minutes later, the old coach rolled down the bottoms of Horse Prairie Creek with the Jehu and shotgun messenger back in their seat. Tugging along behind danced a crazed dun horse. And a couple hundred yards farther back, two slouching riders on dark horses, each wearing a wide-brimmed sombrero and a fancy neckerchief, dogged the lumbering Concord.

For the next two hours, Fortitude worried it out in his head the way he worried a chaw of Bull Durham. He'd gone through Red Rock station a hundred times, but now, when he wanted to conjure up every detail in his head, he could scarcely bring it to his mind's eye. Nothing stood there but a low log cabin, harness shed, and some pens. A haystack. One of the most primitive stations on the Salt Lake trail, actually. Set on the west bank of Red Rock River, right at the crossing. Behind it a way rose a wall of mountains that continued on south. A similar wall lay on the east side of the river. At the south end of the long valley lay Monida Pass, and beyond that the long flats of the Camas Creek country.

The agents would hunker in the cabin, most of them, waiting for the coach to halt. Maybe even waiting for the worn teams to be unhooked and led away. Some might be lying around in wagon beds, or behind the haystack. A lookout or two would spot the coach long before it rolled in; they'd be ready and carefully hidden.

It'd be a good place, isolated and quiet, squarely on the road, and no chance of a detour. Inside the cabin and wagon boxes they'd be protected from his return fire.

"These nags in pretty good shape, Cal?"

"They're some tired. Downhill's the hardest, and twisting downhill even harder still."

"We can't stop at Red Rock. We've got to bull right into the yard and keep on going across the river. Once we ford the river, we got a good chance to run—if these horses have it in them. The agents'll be in the cabin, not mounted. And behind us we got Scrimshaw and Figaro dressed in them neckerchiefs and ready to cover our tail. But it depends on the horses. These'll have to take us to Pleasant Valley or even Camas Creek."

"I'll look after the horses. You worry about the bullets."

"When they see we ain't stopping, they'll shoot, Cal."

Creed spat. "I don't figure they'll be the only ones shooting."

They swung around a vaulting point of rock, and the Red Rock Valley lay before them, the station beyond some cottonwoods, and white in the light of the high moon. Fortitude glanced swiftly at the silent post, and then studied the surrounding ridges, rewarded at last at the faint sight of movement, dull glint in the night. A sentinel.

"This is it, Cal," Hayes said.

"Madre de Dios," whispered Angelica from within.

"Lie low, ma'am, and we'll get you through."

"*Infierno*. I'm going to the *infierno*."

"Don't whup up the team too soon, Cal. Don't give us away until you have to. Make it look like we're about to halt."

"Goddammit, Hayes!"

Fortitude checked behind, gratified to find his riders dogging along one hundred yards back, closing the gap. No way now to tell them what was in store, but they'd read it fast enough and shoot pursuers . . . maybe. A tinhorn gambler in a swallowtail coat and a big farmer.

They drove briefly through cottonwoods, and Fortitude glared tautly into the shadows, expecting trouble. Beyond, a hundred yards off, lay the silent station, its sole window gaping blackly. Horses in the corral. Dull glint of shining leather. Saddled, then, ready for chase. Maybe put buckshot into them. . . .

Nothing. No blue glint of a barrel. Plank door of the cabin shut tight. White smoke curling from the stovepipe. Horses in the corral alert, heads up, facing coach. Haystack, lime green in the moonlight, nothing moving. Two wagons pulled out from yard, down near the crossing, wheels and tongues twisted. From the height of his seat he saw dark bulk in the low beds.

"Watch them wagons, Cal. Dragged down there to flank us if we cross."

He'd have four shotgun blasts to slow them. Two from the sweaty scattergun in his clammy hands, two from the one on the floorboard. He felt scared. The crazy Jehu beside him took the occasion to sit higher, chuck his sombrero back, and spit.

One barrel for the window. One for the door. One for the amassed horses. The other for one of the two wagons. . . .

They rolled into the silent yard now. A penned horse whickered greetings. The Jehu snarled and hawed the team, whipping the wheelers. The coach lurched ahead, throwing Fortitude back. Blue fire spat from the black window and a lead horse staggered. They were shooting the team!

Fortitude squeezed, and the shotgun bucked. Glass shattered and a man screamed. The plank door flew open and shots crackled. Something plucked at Fortitude, smearing pain along his rib cage. Shotgun bucked into his shoulder, and the door slammed shut. Lead horse hit and bucking, swing horse hit and sagging. The coach lurched toward the river. Fire now from the haystack. Shooting from the horse pens. Fortitude yanked up the second shotgun and blew buckshot into the corrals. Horses screeched and bucked.

Shouting now and the clatter of hooves. He glanced behind. Figaro and Scrimshaw racing up, revolvers in hand. A bullet shredded wood inches from him. Down in the coach, Angelica screamed, *"Dios, Dios, Dios, Dios!"*

Men running and dodging, dark forms in white moonlight. The coach lurched down a graveled grade. Lead horses splashing, water silvery, coach careening, almost pitching him off his perch. He grabbed. Beside him that mad Jehu laughing and swearing, booming like a vaudeville basso. Crack of revolvers, snapping lead. From the nearest wagon a rifle barrel coming up. Fortitude swung his shotgun and squeezed—snap, on a dead chamber. He dropped it to the floorboard, and lead smacked wood where his torso had been. He felt giddy and scared wild, couldn't get his revolver out, tugged.

Crack of carbines from the cabin, and a horse shrieked. The other lead horse shuddered. It bucked in the water, splashing, dark gouts of blood spurting from a hole in its neck, rinsed away by water. The horse shivered and fell, dragged along by the momentum of the wheelers and swing horses. Creed yelled, unable to steer the lead team, one dead and the other pain-crazed. A shot smacked Creed's hat off, and it sailed into the river. He laughed wildly and scared the horses. The coach hit a rock and careened on two wheels, the near-side ones clear out of water. Slowly the coach righted itself, wheels splashing, half a ton of gold shifting and sliding in its belly. It settled with a hard snap, the crack of something breaking, and listed leftward.

The living lead horse hit dry land and bucked its way up the gravelly east bank, pushed by panicked horses. Behind, men scurrying for horses, Scrimshaw and the gambler firing deliberately into the corrals, driving the saddled herd into frenzies of pain and terror. Then they raced after the coach, splashing water. Now at last the road agents figured them out and started firing.

A shot plowed into the rump of Scrimshaw's horse. It shuddered and stumbled, rear legs paralyzed, and slid trembling into water. Figaro wheeled to the side and kicked a foot free, while Scrimshaw pulled himself halfway up on Figaro's horse, using the vacated stirrup. They reached the east shore before a rifle shot smacked into their horse, killing it instantly. The bay staggered and sank, and the gambler slid off, while Scrimshaw leapt aside. Ahead of them the coach rumbled, dragging a dead lead horse.

"Whoa up, Cal," cried Hayes.

"Can't stop," he snapped, but somehow he did, tugging on lines, yanking the wheel team lines viciously. The coach sagged to a halt still within effective rifle fire from across the river. Bullets smacked and whined. The coach tilted heavily leftward.

"Thoroughbrace broke!" Creed snarled. "You didn't fix the goddamn thoroughbrace!"

Hayes reloaded the scatterguns, hunkered low. Behind, the gambler and Scrimshaw came running, Scrimshaw limping violently. Bullets plucked at them, scared up dust. But they made small, dark targets in tricky moonlight for marksmen across the black river.

Creed leapt down and cut out the dead lead horse. He tried to free the off-side lead horse, too, but rifle fire from the station drove him back. The dead animal sprawled in dust.

Hayes watched Scrimshaw gain the coach, limping crazily, with Figaro puffing behind. "Don't shoot, Angelica!" he cried.

The coach door swung open and a small revolver cracked viciously from within.

"Dios!" she shrieked, "I shoot him!"

The coach lurched as Scrimshaw tumbled into it, and the gambler a second later. Creed, back on his driver's perch, hawed the crazed team to life. Behind, riders were finally catching the shotgun-frenzied horses in the corrals. Four road agents had mounted and were spurring their mounts toward the river.

Slowly the coach gained momentum, tilted crazily leftward so steeply that Fortitude could scarcely stay on his side of the seat.

In a moment, the riders would catch up and the troubles would begin again, he thought.

"Walk the horses, Cal. Walk 'em so I can aim steady with the Sharps now. It outranges their carbines."

"Slow? Slow? You crazy, Hayes?"

Fortitude crawled up onto the listing coach deck and lay flat, his rifle resting on the rails.

"Tie up the lines, Cal. Git your carcass around and git that six-gun ready, slow and careful," he said.

In the ghostly distance, he saw four mounted men start across the river and race for the fool's coach.

Chapter Fifteen

Four horsemen across the river, hard to see in the moonlight. Fortitude rested the big Sharps on the roof rail, cursing the list of the coach which kept sliding him to the side. His neck hurt where the bullet had nipped it. The crease along his left ribs stung and felt wet. Bleeding slowly, making breath come hard and shooting pain out his arms. His lungs wheezed like torn bellows. The horsemen were still far off, maybe four hundred yards. Blurry, small targets. He squeezed. The heavy rifle bucked into his shoulder, its throating boom tormenting the peace. A horse staggered, pitching its rider.

Shoot the horses. He jammed another paper cartridge in and capped the nipple. They were shooting now, but far out of range, their revolves making small pops in the night. He squeezed deliberately, and a horse somersaulted. He loaded again, feeling the old familiar battle-cool upon him now, and got the third rider's horse, this time apparently a graze because it pitched and bucked rather than going down. He loaded again. The big, solid rifle in his embrace spat lead. He chuckled and fondled it, pain radiating down his arms.

"Oh, you sweet baby" he muttered. "Oh, you beautiful mother!"

But he had only a handful of the paper cartridges left. The remaining pursuer had had enough and pulled up. More horsemen splashed across the ford now, fifty yards farther back. Fortitude rested the reloaded weapon on the rail again, cursed the tilting coach, and fired, seeing a geyser of moonlit water erupt just beyond his target. They didn't like it; he could see that. Four paused in the middle of the river. He fired into the middle of them, hitting a horse and starting the others bucking and pitching riders into the water. None of them wanted to tangle with a Sharps that threw .60-caliber balls a hundred yards farther than their own weapons. They retreated, at least for the moment, back into the station yard.

The retreat galvanized those in the coach. Scrimshaw ducked out of the door and unharnessed the wounded lead horse, leaving four. Of these, two were grazed and half crazy.

Calvin Creed tugged his gauntlets back on and clambered to his seat, cursing. "This coach leans so bad I can't stay put up here," he growled. "You should have fixed the thoroughbrace."

"Looked all right," Hayes muttered. "Just sat in water too long at the mudslide."

"I can't hardly drive around a curve without this coach tipping over and me with it," Creed muttered.

Hayes walked over to the side of the coach. On the near side, the great leather leafspring that cradled the coach body had pulled apart near the rear axle. He couldn't imagine how to fix it. The cant of the coach body would bind the left front wheel anytime Creed turned the coach left. It'd have to do; they couldn't abandon the coach. Maybe when they got to a cottonwood grove they could jam a pole under there, resting on the axles, coach body on the pole.

"Let's git," he muttered, swinging up beside Creed. The cant slid him into the low corner of the seat. "You better sit here, Cal, else you slide down from the high side with hands full of lines."

They traded places and Creed hawed the teams. The coach creaked forward, squeaking and scraping weirdly. Fortitude squinted out into the moon-swept night, noting that horsemen were spreading out on the far side of the river, intending to shadow the coach and maybe pounce when the moon set and they made poorer targets. Actually, even across the river they remained within range, and probably knew it, but he wasn't going to waste precious cartridges now.

"They'll git ahead and try it again," he said. "Find a mess of cottonwoods, hunker down and not worry about this here big Sharps. I don't figure we got much time, especially with that moon sliding downhill."

From within the coach Scrimshaw spoke up. "When the moon sets, we've got darkness on our side. Maybe we can hide."

Creed guffawed. "Hide a coach," he said.

Hayes didn't say anything, but Scrimshaw's notion intrigued him.

"We got any sharp left turns ahead, Cal? Near wheel's going to bind on the coach body."

"Not for ten miles," he said. "Closer we get toward Monida Pass, the more the road twists."

Across the river, ghostly horsemen forged ahead and vanished over a low ridge. It gave Hayes a notion.

"Do you suppose they got anyone shading us behind?" he asked, obscure excitement in his voice. "Did all them agents slip out ahead of us?"

From within the coach, Figaro spoke: "Nothing visible on my side."

They hit bad ruts, and the coach groaned and squealed ominously, the body banging into the front wheel.

"Hayes?" said Scrimshaw. "All these valises have slid downhill. Piling against the canvas wall we lashed up. One good bounce and they'll rip through, all over the ground."

That did it. "Cal, slow down," Fortitude said. "Give them another few minutes to git on ahead. Then we'll git back to Red

Rock. This coach is done for, and I've a mind to switch to them two wagons back there and free up old Hospers—if he's still alive. Maybe there's even stuff around to fix this coach, but I doubt it."

"I don't feature driving some two-bit wagon to Fort Hall," retorted Creed stiffly.

"Damned Jehu," Hayes muttered, and Creed guffawed, slowing the coach.

Fortitude peered around sharply. The roll of the hill lay ahead, and the road agents had galloped beyond it, out of sight. Nothing. No shadowing riders across the river or to the rear.

"Turn, Cal," he snapped.

The Jehu swung into a wide right loop over sloped prairie, and the coach thumped ominously, threatening to tip and spill the half ton of treasure in its hold. Delicately Creed swung it around, his gauntleted hands masterful in their command of the edgy team, and in a moment they rumbled north toward Red Rock station, and the low moon lay behind them.

Hayes scrambled out upon the canted roof again to cover their rear, half expecting the agents to boil over the crest of the frost-whitened hill that hid them. He had six paper cartridges in his pocket and one chambered.

The coach creaked and groaned, and the near-side wheels squealed under the unusual load on them. The remaining thoroughbrace twanged and stuttered. It was all that kept the tilted Concord body from toppling sideways.

"Come on, baby," Hayes muttered.

Creed took it for a command and set the horses into a smart trot while the coach lurched drunkenly behind, rattling and screaming through the night on tormented wheels. They hit a pothole that jammed the deck into Hayes's ribs, and the coach crashed sickeningly.

"Goddammit, Cal," Hayes snarled.

Creed guffawed, snapped the lines, murdering the fool's coach, bouncing passengers and gold about.

Still the Concord held together.

"*Madre de Dios,*" cried Angelica. "You will kill us. The gold, it landed on my leg."

Creed bayed at the moon. "And the driving is like the driving of Jehu the son of Nimshi: for he driveth furiously," he howled.

They struck the ford at a gallop, and the coach careened wildly, forcing Fortitude to clutch rifle and shotguns with one hand and the coachwork with the other. Water geysered up, dashing him with ice while Cal Creed bawled and bayed and jerked the careening coach to an abrupt halt before the black station.

They were all too stunned and appalled to say anything.

The horses shook and snorted in their traces, spraying water.

The driver tucked his gauntlets into his broad belt with a flourish and stepped down.

Hayes snatched at his revolver and studied the hushed station, the opened door, the gaping, shattered window, two sprawled horses in the corral—and a body lying with limbs akimbo near the haystack.

"Creed, you idjit," Hayes muttered. Still, the night lay quiet. Then, from within the blackened log station, a groan.

Below him, Hayes heard the hickory coach door squeak open.

"Don't take nothing for granted," he muttered as Scrimshaw and Figaro stepped out, revolvers in hand.

"Go search them wagons and corrals and such," he added. "You got good pins. I'll see who's in here."

He slid cautiously off the seat, chest pain searing him. Creed had wandered off nonchalantly, looking for horses, he supposed. He doubted any were left, except maybe some injured ones.

Angelica started out the coach door, but Hayes shooed her back in. "You just wait until we look it all over, ma'am."

"I do not wait much longer," she said, ignoring him and heading toward the necessary rooms off to the rear. At least she had that little pepperbox in hand, he thought.

"You inside," said Hayes quietly. "Come out with your hands high or face what's coming."

"I can't. My leg's busted. Horse fell on it."

"Throw your revolver out."

"Don't have any."

"Who else is in there?"

"Just me—alive."

"Who's dead?"

No answer.

Hayes crept to a point beside the door, flattening himself against the log wall.

"Tell me again who's in there—" he began, and sprang through into the station, dropping low in the blackness.

"Don't shoot!" came the voice.

Hayes let his eyes adjust to the gloom. Moonlight filtered in, revealing two hulks across the clay floor. One moved.

He sprang again, landing near the moving one, finding the man's arms and hands, and no weapon. The man groaned.

Satisfied, Hayes contemplated the other unmoving bulk, sensing death, and then risked a lucifer. The flaring light revealed a sprawled, dead Hospers, and a living man staring in terror into the bore of Hayes's revolver.

The match died.

"Who are you?"

The bearded man fell silent.

"Who rode ahead? Thought I saw George Ives—that blond hair. You fellas didn't even bother with masks," he said. "I guess that says something about what you were fixin' to do to us." He flourished the revolver. "Talk!"

"I'm innocent!"

"Talk or I'll squeeze. My finger's getting right itchy."

"You wouldn't kill a man in cold blood!"

"I suppose Hospers died of old age," Hayes retorted. "My name's Hayes. What's yours?"

The man fainted, or pretended to. Hayes kicked him, evoked a groan but not consciousness. It didn't matter.

So they'd killed Hospers, he thought. A tough old bird, bent like a question mark, who handled the station alone mostly, some ancient bitterness in his bright blue eyes and a mouth curled downward under the white stubble of his occasionally shaved face. They'd shot him in cold blood and left him sprawled beside the tin stove. He'd be a witness, so they'd murdered him without a second thought. Fortitude wished he could bury the old buzzard and say some words. Maybe later. He didn't even know Hospers' first name. It had always been Hospers, one name, reliable with fresh drays harnessed and waiting in the pen, run after run.

Hayes stalked out of the stinking black station into the clear white night just as Scrimshaw and Figaro approached.

"One dead. Small fry I saw in Churchill's. I don't know his name. Mostly he stayed in Bannack," Figaro said crisply.

"One dead horse in the corrals, two down but alive, one crazed one in a corner. Nothing around the haystack. Nothing in the wagons. I guess we didn't do them much harm," Aristotle said.

"Didn't expect to," Hayes said. "They maybe took some injured with them getting ahead of us. What about the wagons?"

"One's got a tongue and doubletree. Two-horse wagon for the gold. The other's a one-horse with shafts."

Hayes felt exhausted, and his wounds screamed at him. The others looked ready to drop. But there was no time. Never any time.

"Creed," he bawled. "We got work to do. Drive this coach over to them wagons and put the gold in the two-horse."

Wordlessly Creed clambered up to the tilted seat and coaxed the team the few yards to the wagons, and sat waiting.

Hayes knew better than to ask Creed to help with the sweaty work. "You watch for surprises, Cal," he muttered.

They sliced open the canvas side of the coach and yanked fiercely at the valises and saddlebags. Each seemed nailed to the floor. Hayes felt his bad leg giving under him, and cursed.

"I can't do it," he muttered.

Figaro couldn't do it, either. Long years of playing cards and shoving chips didn't equip him for it. That left Scrimshaw, who stared wearily at the mound of baggage and began hauling it to the wagon, glaring bitterly at Creed, who wedged himself up on the seat and tugged importantly at his gauntlets.

"Hide this thing behind the station—better yet, off in them cottonwoods," Hayes snapped. Damned Jehu.

He glared wearily at the surrounding hills. The white moon had turned gold and hung fatly just above the western mountains. In ten minutes the night would turn pitch-black, and that suited Fortitude just fine.

On the shadowed porch, he made out the black figure of Angelica.

"I am so tired," she said. "I was a fool—this foolish trip."

"You're alive and we still got your gold," Hayes retorted angrily. He hated that kind of talk. What did they expect—a lark?

"But the *bandidos* are all ahead," she retorted. "I am sick of gold."

He ignored her, his mind on the trip ahead. They'd be riding through a bitter night. They were all starved. He limped over to the dead coach and pulled the buffalo robes from it.

"Find axes and shovels," he said to Figaro. "And rope. Maybe we'll just make our own road. And a tarp, if there's one."

The gambler nodded and began poking around the coach yard and the open-sided shed. Hayes headed back to to the log station, looking for other things. A wave of dizziness caught him, buckled him over for a minute. It passed. He found a lamp and lit it. Empty gun rack. No ammunition. The wounded road agent on the clay floor stirred. Hayes watched him a moment.

Food. This station didn't feed passengers. Strictly a horse stop. Hospers had rigged a kitchen of sorts against the wall where his body lay, next to the tin stove. Filthy planks, a grimy dry sink. Flour and sugar and coffee beans in tin canisters, but the agents had stripped the place of anything immediately edible.

A sack of pinto beans. They couldn't take time to cook here. He found a burlap bag and piled food into it, along with a greasy black frying pan, the two tin plates, and two spoons and knife that apparently were the sum of Hospers' utensils. The tin stuff rattled in the bag, and Hayes frowned.

The moon vanished, plunging the place into an ethereal darkness. At the wagons he found Scrimshaw tugging at a rope.

"I've pulled the tarp over the gold and lashed it all down," the young man said. "Won't bounce out now, even if the wagon rolls."

"One more thing," said Hayes. "Find the tar pot and grease them wheels, all of them. I don't want these wagons squeaking and howling through the night. We're going to try to sneak around. Leave the tar pot in the wagon."

Even in the dark, he could see a tired grin on Scrimshaw's face.

"I'll do it, Sergeant," the young man said.

It took a few minutes more for Creed to drive the groaning coach back into the cottonwoods and unhitch the two spans of horses. They harnessed the two better ones to the gold wagon, backed a crease-crazed one between the shafts of the other wagon, and tied the remaining draft horse—the one with the furrow along the stifle—behind as a spare. It shrieked.

Fortitude Hayes wrestled with an idea and returned to the black cabin, his revolver in hand. That wounded son of a bitch should die. He stalked in. Without moonlight in the windows, the interior lay pitch-black before him.

"You!" he snarled, hating this.

No answer.

He stalked to where the wounded man should be, found him with his boot, and kicked. An explosion of bad breath. He kicked again, evoking a groan. His arms trembled and ached.

He aimed the revolver and couldn't pull the trigger. Angrily he backed out into the starlight, mad at himself. That son of a bitch deserved a ball. He was getting soft. He raged at himself, at the wounded man, at road agents in general, road agents who'd killed a hundred travelers in these parts. A hundred at least—and Hospers, too. He slumped into the porch support for a minute, unable to stand, and then stalked toward the wagons, muttering furiously.

Creed elected to drive the gold, and mounted the battered wagon with a flourish, tugging on his gauntlets exactly as he did before admiring audiences at stage stops.

"These seats ain't padded," Creed bawled. "I don't know why I'm doing this."

Hayes laughed nastily and crawled in beside Scrimshaw, who held the lines. On the seat behind, Angelica huddled in a filthy blanked she'd commandeered from the cabin, and the sporting man sat calmly under a moth-eaten buffalo robe.

Hayes made one last check. On the floorboards at his feet lay the shotguns. Across his lap, the Sharps. He felt dizzy and peered into the starlit faces around him, seeing sheer exhaustion. They were all tottering on their last legs, and yet they had a tough run to make before dawn.

"We'll quit the road and stay on the west side of the river," he said. "I reckon the agents are across the stream and waiting for the coach on the other side. Maybe if we're lucky we can slip by and stay on this side clear to Monida Pass. These wagons'll go where a coach can't."

No one argued. No one complained. No one said he was tired or hungry or cold. No one said he was afraid for his life. That was the last thing he remembered.

Chapter Sixteen

Blood still oozed from Fortitude's ribs. He'd lost a lot. It lay caked on his purplish flesh, brown in the lamplight. No one had known: his heavy mackinaw had hidden the wound.

They stared at her, expecting her to fix him. But she didn't know anything about this. She was not a doctor. She stared up at them from the filthy floor of the way station, seeing their exhausted faces.

"Build up the fire and heat water," she said wearily. "So I can *lave*—wash. He's full of blood, yes?"

They were all strangers, these tired men. If Fortitude Hayes died . . . But he wouldn't die. He breathed regularly, his mouth open and his beard straining cold air. Filthy. Everything here was filthy.

"Lift him to the *cama*—bed."

Scrimshaw gently lifted the old shotgun messenger to the grimy bunk, stepping gingerly past the road agent with the broken leg, who stared silently in the yellow light.

"Pronto, pronto," she cried angrily. The sporting man found

some wood and threw it over the coals in the battered stove. They cracked and spat, startling them.

"We're not going anywhere, Creed. Help me with the gold," said Scrimshaw.

"I'm just off my sickbed, young man."

The haggard miner stared, and sagged. "I don't have the strength left," he muttered. "Just loaded all of it into the wagon a few minutes ago."

"I'll help in a minute. After I get some water," the gambler said, disappearing into the night with a battered pail.

Off in the far corner, Hospers' body lay, an evil presence in the station. "Take him away pronto, *por favor,*" she said.

She began to slip into Spanish, as she always did when she'd reached the end of her strength.

Scrimshaw tumbled in, dragging two of her valises. She stared at her gold, hating it. Because of it, this man beside her on the foul bunk lay wounded. And all of them were at their limits. She watched dully as he let the bags crash into the clay floor and plunged out into the bitter night again.

"What if they come? No one is watching," she said aloud, but no one heard. She addressed the wounded *bandido* on the floor. "Maybe you will die for gold. Like I die for gold."

He didn't respond.

Creed vanished into the night, and she heard the movement of horses. He was unharnessing them, leading them down to the river for a drink and putting them out into the paddock.

So! she thought. No horses! Here they would wait for the road agents to return. *Here she would die!*

The gambler started water heating and walked wearily into the night to help unload the wagons.

Ah! she thought. He will die, too. And he came only to save his life, not for the filthy gold. He should live. If God sits on his throne, the gambler should live. Scrimshaw returned, dragging one of his saddlebags. It seemed heavier than her valises, and he could barely scrape it along the clay. The gambler entered, white-faced and panting, a valise in his hand. He dropped it with a heavy thump.

Nobody watches, she thought. She stood and walked out into the harsh night, her little pepperbox, carefully reloaded, in hand. She couldn't see anything. The night lay inky before her, and behind, the yellow lanternlight cast long, dim streaks across the yard. Stars had vanished behind some black cloud mass, making the night opaque and impenetrable. Maybe it had become too dark for the road agents to ride, but she doubted that. They'd come soon. They'd come hunting for the coach, long delayed now. Maybe here already, watching all this weary activity, gathering for the final murderous stroke.

Out at the corrals she heard horses cough and shift restlessly, and then Creed appeared in the light, in the bores of her pepperbox. *Dios!* She might have shot him!

The sporting man cleaned the last things from the wagon, Hayes's weapons, the burlap bag of food, the robes.

"You stay here—in the blackness—and watch, yes?" she said. "You maybe take a scattergun. Soon they come, yes?"

He nodded and picked up one of the shotguns, stationing himself in shadow.

Scrimshaw had somehow managed to empty the two-horse wagon of the gold and drag it all into the station. She'd never seen a man so tired and haggard. He slumped, panting, near the lamp.

"One more thing," she said softly. "The dead man. The station *jefe*."

Scrimshaw grimaced fleetingly and picked up Hospers gently, carrying him out into the night. Angelica blessed herself as the dead man passed by. Made the sign of the cross against spirits and devils and the darkness.

"Maybe soon we carry you out into the night," she said crossly to the injured road agent.

"Water," he rasped.

She filled a dipper and let him slurp it up.

The water on the stove remained lukewarm to her finger. She wrestled Fortitude's flannel shirt off and jerked down his britches.

Brown blood caked his thigh. The crease along the front of his left ribs lay open and ugly. The flesh around it looked purple and black in the dim light. It might mortify if she didn't wash it well. Wounded for her gold, hurt for her gold, maybe more death. *Muerte!* But he breathed regularly, groaning whenever she poked and probed.

Behind her, Scrimshaw closed and barred the shutters, forting up. It wouldn't stop a dozen or so road agents long. He collapsed wearily onto a wooden bench, too worn to do more.

"They'll catch us all in here," he muttered. "We're too done in even to keep a watch. I can't stay awake anymore. I'm fighting it every second."

From out on the porch, the sporting man spoke. "I'll watch," he said softly. "You sleep. Get your rest. Eat first."

"You've been up longer than the rest of us, I hear."

"A gambler learns to ignore his body," Figaro replied. "I've sat through three-day poker games, never sleeping. Hardly even taking time to—to take care of needs."

Creed returned. "Horses taken care of," he muttered. "Only one good one. Found wounds on the rest. All half crazy or bled down to weakness. We couldn't have gotten far even if Fortitude'd been all right. . . . Might have pulled that Concord a mile or so."

He closed the heavy door and started to bar it.

"Don't. The professor's out there, watching," muttered Scrimshaw.

"He falls asleep and the road agents walk right in," grumbled Creed.

"Maybe two of us should watch. I can last a while longer."

She ignored them. The water had come up to heat, and she lifted the kettle to the corner of the stove. Not a clean cloth anywhere except in her travel bag. She dug in it, found a chemise, and began rinsing blood from Fortitude's torso. He groaned whenever water slid into the long wound.

"Maybe Professor Figaro, maybe he stands in the dark to let the agents come in without a fight," she said, rinsing Hayes.

She felt Scrimshaw standing over her, dark as thunder.

"Why do you say that?"

"He's got no gold."

"Hayes said his life is in danger."

She shrugged. "No gold. Maybe you got no gold. Rocks in those bags. You never show me."

"I haven't seen your gold, either. Your whore's gold."

"I will show it! And you will show me yours!"

He sagged. "No, I believe you. I'm trusting you, a whore. I'm trusting him, a tinhorn. Crooked two-bit riverboat gambler who never earned an honest dollar in his life. Your type looks for easy pickings; you're both vultures. Feasting on hardworking men. You lie on your back and get rich. He deals too fast and gets rich. You're both takers, not givers. You don't build, you don't add to a place. You don't *work*. Road agents don't *work*. You suck the lifeblood out of it, like these road agents—that might just be your partners. I don't trust you, but I trust Hayes. He said—he said . . . you're safe. But if you or that other lowlife try anything, I'll—I'll . . ." The tired miner couldn't seem to finish his threat.

"I am sorry," she said. Then, softly, "I am not what you say. *Puta*. I never sell myself. I go now to make a proper life and confess to a padre and go to Mass each day. You don't care any, but it is so."

"Quit running these people down, Scrimshaw," snarled Creed. "They're all better'n you, if you want to know. They got courage. All you got is a narrow mind and a way of working your fingers off. It don't honor life much to muck like a slave and run from whatever scares you."

Scrimshaw reddened but didn't reply. He slumped deeper on the bench, burying his face in his big hands. "I'm tired," he muttered. It came close to an apology, but fell short.

She finished sponging Fortitude Hayes. He lay inert, white and wheezing, and she wondered when he'd come to. He'd lost blood, and a little still seeped from the crease. She peered around the station, looking for something, anything, to keep it from mortifying. On a shelf sat a tin gallon of turpentine. She'd never used it, but she'd heard of it. Some of her girls had used it for cuts.

Wearily she pulled it down and uncapped it. The acrid smell assaulted her. Anything that smelled so bad would be good, she knew. She poured it into the crease, and Sergeant Hayes shrieked, his body bucking on the bunk.

The others came awake, staring at her.

"Help me bind him up now," she said primly. "I bind him up so the road agents can shoot him later."

The tic spasming his left eyelid wouldn't go away, and grew annoying to Professor Figaro. It had started when young Scrimshaw spouted off about lowlifes, his voice carrying through the shutters. The professor had never doubted where he and Angelica stood with that young prig, even before the outburst. But the words had sliced deep anyway and started his eyelid jerking.

He slouched on the bench along the front of the station, much the way old Hospers had whiled away hours and days, waiting for the coaches to come and go. The night had turned bitter, but he felt reasonably comfortable wrapped in his buffalo robe and stamping his numb feet occasionally. A vast cloud mass blotted the stars and the high dome of the sky, turning the night thick. When the stars shone, it had seemed transparent and clear and friendly. Now it felt heavy and walled. He could barely make out the roof of the porch or the edges of the building behind him.

By force of concentration and long habit, he willed aside the weariness of his body. He knew how to ignore his body and its clamor. In fact, he usually won marathon poker games when the bodies of other players began to betray them, and behind their hooded eyes and frozen gazes he sensed their squirming desperation and waited for their mistakes. So he sat, a shotgun in hand under the robe, and ignored everything except what his ears, nose, and eyes registered.

Several times he sensed a presence in the night. Once a horse in the corral snorted. Another time he thought he heard the fall of hoof on frozen ground. Occasionally the gurgle of Red Rock River lifted to him, and he hoped it wouldn't mask more significant noise.

Aristotle Scrimshaw's type of censure was common enough, and he'd heard versions of his moralizing for years. It never quite bounced off the professor the way it should, because he discerned some truth in it. Sitting comfortably in his chair, living high, he'd skinned away the hard-won dust of countless grubbing miners, dust ripped from icy streams with backbreaking labor. It didn't particularly bother him. No man had to sit down at his tables or pick up the cards he dealt.

He'd been a square player, but innocents like Scrimshaw wouldn't know that. The others, the sporting bloods, the ones who frequented his tables and other tables, knew it. But innocents never fathomed it, never fathomed that the professor had all the edge he needed from his poker skills, or the house advantage in games. In any case, Professor Figaro looked crooked as the devil's trident, his mouth twisted and his gaze sneaky when he played.

But for all of that, Scrimshaw's censure irked him. A woman like Angelica, wanting only quiet respectability, meant nothing to Scrimshaw. Randolph Figaro's own youthful tragedy and the way the cards fell afterward—that would mean nothing to Scrimshaw, either. His world had bleached all black and white. It was full of builders and parasites, good and evil, and once anyone crossed the line, there would be no getting back.

Well, the miner would be asleep now in the darkened building, sleeping the sleep of the righteous. The professor wiggled his toes, bringing life into them. He'd have to last until dawn. No telling what tomorrow might bring. A siege probably. Death. Unless a coach rolled in or a freight outfit relieved them. Not that freighters hauled much this late in the season. . . .

"You."

The low voice rose from his left, startling him.

"You. slow and quiet, put your gun down and stand. If you shoot, you're dead."

Randolph Figaro sat stone still. So, they'd come after all, working through the blackest of nights. But did they really see him? He sat in a dark buffalo robe he couldn't see himself. They wouldn't see his black hair, either, but maybe his face. They were probing, fishing. Slowly he lifted the shotgun under the robe.

"You come out from under that porch, you son of a bitch." The voice buzzed as low as a bumblebee's hum.

They didn't know where he was, then, or they'd not want him out of the shadow. He waited quietly, worrying about the unbarred door. These agents could simply walk in and take the gold and kill the rest without a fight.

Professor Figaro could see nothing. He didn't even sense the presence of others. He had worked saloons and salons all his life, and the rhythms of the outdoors were alien to him. He might fire the shotgun and kill one or two, but the flash would tell them where he sat—and he'd be riddled in seconds. They'd be through the door in seconds, too. He needed to wake them up inside, give them a chance to fortify. So he sat silently. He couldn't pull the shotgun barrel up under his robe, but he could ready his revolver. He slid his free left hand into the pocket of his swallowtail coat, clutched the small weapon, and lifted it.

"Let's rush. Knock that door in," came a low voice from the right.

"Shhh!"

"Door may be barred. Walk right into guns."

"They're asleep."

"Burn it. Gold don't burn."

"The bags will, spill dust all to hell. Roof caves in on the dust and we won't even get at it for hours. Maybe lose it."

"You want to go knockin' on the door, nice and polite?"

"Let's see a minute," someone replied.

The professor identified three voices, left and center. Nothing to his right as far as he could tell. He knew one voice, and it made him sweat. George Ives.

He could, he thought, walk straight out into the night and they wouldn't know the difference. Maybe even shoot at them from the rear, from around the corrals or haystack somewhere. A shotgun blast and then drop. They could scarcely target him in a darkness like this. He tried hard to remember where the wagons were. They could trip him up.

He heard a whisper of movement to his right and the squawk of a protesting board on his left. Creeping toward the door, then. Not seeing, but feeling their way. Seconds left. Once they gained the door and pushed . . .

He saw clearly how it would be. The hock card.

"You," came the whispered voice. "We see you now. Hands up slow and easy, and you'll live. All we want's the gold. Where is it? Just inside the door?"

Professor Figaro said nothing. His best chance, his only chance, was to stand slowly, take two steps to the right, slip quickly inside, and drop the bolt before they rushed. He shrugged off the robe, hearing it fall heavily. He stood. Took one soft step. Then another. The door loomed behind him. He shifted back into the door frame, feeling somewhat protected now from gunshot from either side, shifted back until his shoulder blades pressed into the whipsawed plank of the door. One good shove and he'd be in, he thought. He'd have to be agile, slam the door, and drop the bolt. Where was the bolt, right or left of the door? He couldn't remember.

He tensed, poised to push back. From within, a loud thump, harsh in the night. He rammed back into solid wood, unforgiving wood. They'd bolted it! Shock ran through him like ice water. Bolted him out!

Footfall along the porch now, on the left. One of them coming. Some instinct told him to drop low, and he did, sliding down to his knees, whipping the cumbersome shotgun around, pointing left, the weapon tucked under his arm instead of at his shoulder.

The explosion deafened him. The shotgun bucked violently, twisting him, ripping the weapon out of his grasp. Someone screamed. The shotgun clattered. Hoarse cries, men running. He scrambled straight out into the night, felt bodies pounding by, heard the slam of flesh upon the barred door. Now blue flashes stabbed the night. He raced to the right now, to where he thought the haystack might be, the corrals, though he could see nothing.

He tripped on something and sprawled, skinning a knee, ripping his fine trousers. He didn't find the haystack, but did find the river, stopping at the last moment when the ripple of water alerted him. From all sides of the station, gun flashes lacerated the night, aimless shots thumping log and plank. From within, nothing. He wasn't sure whether the building had loopholes or not. Probably not. They'd be trapped behind plank shutters and plank door and log, no way to shoot back.

Professor Figaro lay on the frosty ground, heart tripping, feeling the bitterness of the night seep through him. Bolted the door and locked him out! He wondered who had dropped that bolt. Scrimshaw? Whoever it was didn't give a damn about him. Betrayed him. They were all guilty, except Hayes. Hayes didn't do it. Not old Fortitude. He sighed. On a night like this he could probably stumble his way to some hiding place, escape the road agents, who'd get their gold, kill everyone inside, and ride off. Maybe fate had dealt him a flush hand, he thought, surprised by all this. Walk away. He still had his revolver, not to mention his derringer. Walk away. He had two decks of cards, his swallowtail coat, his patent leather shoes, and his dust and greenback bank. Not to mention his life and health. He had a few lucifers, a small knife, and his headlight diamond stickpin on his cravat. He lacked only a good fat Havana cigar. . . .

From around the station, flame stabbed and lead smacked into plank and wall, picking at chinks. Walk away. A royal flush. He laughed shortly, enjoying the calm seeping into his rattled head and the peace sweeping through his taut body. With half-numb fingers he checked the caps on the nipples of his revolver, and then began to ease toward the left, where men muttered profanely and loosed carbine shots into log walls.

Chapter Seventeen

The thump and smack of gunfire sucked Fortitude Hayes out of some vast void. He listened, identifying the crack of carbines, the pop of revolvers, the shrill smack of lead plowing into log and plank. Nearby he heard a woman sobbing.

He opened his eyes and saw utterly nothing. Not the faintest light to give murky shape to things. On a bed. He felt a straw-filled tick rustling under him. And a bedbug skinning along a thigh. And the itch of several bites. And some silky fabric pinning his ribs tight across a streak of pain.

"Am I blind?" he muttered.

"*Dios!* It is you."

"My eyes. Did they get my eyes?"

From across a void, Creed's voice: "Naw, Hayes. It's just plain black in here. Moon's down. Whole sky's got heavy cloud over it, and spitting a bit of ice. No one can see nothing."

Fortitude listened to the desultory shooting. "Who's here?" he said. "Where's that road agent with the busted leg?"

He tried to lift himself off the bunk, but fell back dizzily. Too much blood lost, and thirsty as hell.

"Figaro's out. Rest of us in," said Creed. "He didn't make it in time. I had to bar the door when they sneaked in."

His tone sounded defensive. Anger flared in Hayes.

"Did you open up and reach for him first, Creed?"

Silence.

"So they got him," Hayes muttered angrily. "Where's that busted-leg son of a bitch? Strike a lucifer!"

Creed did, and in the wild white flare Hayes saw everything he needed to see. The road agent had dragged himself almost to the door. In moments, he would have pulled himself up and lifted the bar. Creed saw it, too, and snarled, landing on the man catlike and hauling him back.

A thud, a shriek, and groaning.

In the renewed dark, Hayes snarled at the road agent. "The first shot gets fired in here goes into your skull, buster."

No answer. He sorted out the other impressions garnered from a single flare of a sulfur match. Scrimshaw sprawled out, dead to the world, unaware of the shooting. Angelica near the stove, weeping into her hands. Gold mounded just inside the barred door, where it had been dragged.

"Cal," he snapped. "Pull that gold away from the door. Drag it under the bunk here, and do it in the dark."

"Why should I—"

"Move!"

He heard the muttering Jehu tug at bags, and the scrape of leather over filthy clay, and then the wheeze of the man as he approached.

"Angelica," he said softly. "I need water. Plumb dry after losing so much juice. And then find me my revolver and belt. Feel better with iron in my hand."

She didn't reply, but moments later he felt his bunk sag with her weight, and he found the dipper with his hands and drank it all, icy water slaking need and cooling his fever. She handed him his gun belt, and he grasped the weapon.

"Wake Scrimshaw. He should be dragging this gold of his," muttered Creed.

Fortitude thought about it. The young man had folded, and not even a splash of water in his stubbled face would bring him around.

"Let him be awhile," Fortitude said.

"Let him be? With this place going under, and them agents fixing to kill us, batter the shutters in, or chop that door?"

Creed sounded outraged.

"Angelica, is there fire in the stove?" Fortitude asked.

"Only coals. You want—"

"No. Throw a little water in. Just a little. Put it out."

"But it's *frío*—cold."

"First thing they'll try is plugging the chimney and smoking us out."

He heard the rustle of her skirts, and the sudden hiss. Acrid steam rolled across the frigid air.

"We will all be dead," she muttered. "All for gold."

"Hush!" Hayes snapped. Then, gently, "You're too hard on yourself, Angelica. Never lookin' to see what's next in your life. Don't you worry about such things now. Just think that we're in this together, Scrimshaw's gold is here, too, and we'll help you all we can."

His sergeant mind began sorting things out, as it always somehow did under fire. Figaro lost. Dead or wounded. Road agents outside, pasting the station with lead—because they didn't know what to do. Batter down the door and rush in? Into pitch black; no targets. Burn it? Sod roof collapsing on the gold. Leather pokes burned and dust scattered, and all too hot, an inferno, orange embers. Much too hot, and road traffic coming in the morning, coaches, freight trains, no time to let it all cool down. . . . Still, they'd think of something. More gold than they'd ever seen here. Something. . . .

"You got the shotguns, Cal?" he asked.

"Yes."

"That's all we need," Fortitude said. "Ideal for this."

Creed snorted.

"You have any notion of the hour? How long to dawn?" Fortitude asked.

"No idea."

"Tell me about the horses, Cal."

"Only one that wasn't hurt. The rest of the drays all got holes or scrapes, ringy as hell."

"Where are the road-agent cayuses?"

"Never heard a one. First thing I knew, there was soft talk, threats against Figaro out front, real close. So I dropped—"

"You threw him to the wolves, Creed."

From outside, a sharp voice: "Hayes. Throw us the gold and we'll leave. Otherwise you're all dead."

Hayes didn't reply. Nothing to say.

From the blackness, the road agent on the floor cried out, "No, George. This is Perk. They got me in here. Don't—don't—"

A strange wild laughter erupted beyond the plank door.

"That's Ives," muttered Creed. "I heard that laugh before, once when he held us up, burlap bag over his head."

"Remember me, George," cried the road agent.

Hayes heard a thump and scream. Creed had done something.

"You in there. Hayes!" came the voice again. "We got your man here. Feels like Professor Figaro, but we ain't sure. Tinhorns bleed as fast as anyone else, maybe faster. You open up the door and toss out the gold or we'll shoot him. I'll count to three, Hayes."

Silence. Hayes waited.

"One!"

"*Dios,* do something, señor! They will kill him!"

"Two."

Creed coughed. Fortitude waited for a voice. If the professor was alive, he'd be bleating.

From outside, crazy laughter, a giggle that sent shivers through him.

"Three, Hayes!" The blast of a revolver racketed in, followed by two more blasts, and wild laughter and a thump on the porch.

That thump. Fortitude sagged. Maybe they killed Figaro after all while he was half-conscious, propped up for the bullet. Maybe he'd just let a man be killed for the goddamned gold.

Angelica sobbed. "*Asesino*. Murderer! He good man, *inocente*!"

"Hoax, Angelica. Figaro would have hollered." He wasn't sure of that himself, and felt bad, some terrible hollow guilt down within. He tried to rise up, but dizziness drove him back again.

She sobbed and choked, certain of death. "Señor Hayes," she wept. "Gladly I would give up my gold. I hate it! I hate it! It murders us. It kills me!"

"Need another dipper of water, Angelica."

Thumping above them now, treading on the sod roof, muffled in the icy black. Scrape of a shovel. Pulling away sod. Soon they'd take an ax to the rough-sawn plank, probably drop firebrands inside so they could target everyone. . . . Then bust the shutters.

"Cal. The Sharps."

"Around here somewhere," the Jehu muttered. "Here!"

"Angelica. Wake up Scrimshaw. Slap him if you have to."

"Give them my gold! Give them my gold!" she cried.

"Wake him."

He heard a splash and muttering, and a small woman's voice poking and probing and crooning and sobbing.

"Let me be . . ." muttered Aristotle.

Above, the shovel scratched wood. Scraping sounds, a thump. Smack of an ax, shuddering wood, squealing plank. Splintering.

Cal struck a match. Overhead the glint of an ax head piercing wood. As the match died, the iron head vanished. Creed lifted the Sharps, angling it the way the ax had fallen, and fired. An incredible blast inside the station. Acrid powder smoke. Ringing ears. From above, a yell and silence.

Fortitude strained to listen.

"You try it," came a muffled voice.

"Not me! I ain't getting my head blowed off."

Then silence, and the thump of retreating boots.

Not long to daylight, Fortitude thought. And when it came, the outlaws would have all the advantages. For a while anyway, until traffic rolled in.

"They're here," muttered Scrimshaw in the dark. "Where's my gun? I can't think yet. I never even fell asleep."

"Your turn, Aristotle. Cal, you get some rest."

"You good and awake, Scrimshaw?" Cal asked. "They're trying stuff."

Hayes sat up, letting the dizziness wash over him, past him. The water had helped. "Take the bunk, Cal. I'm up now."

Cal Creed didn't argue. Hayes felt the driver brush by and sag into the tick. He stood shakily in the blackness. The station stank of sweat and fear and ancient tobacco. And fresh urine.

"Aristotle, I got work for you. I want a loophole on each side, but especially on the front, high—so high we got to stand on a table or chair to use one. Higher than they can reach out there. You're handy. You got the skills to knock out the chinking—pretty big holes. I'm too weak and Creed's a goddamn Jehu. I'm going to light the lamp for a minute while you find stuff—tools, hammer, chisel, whatever."

"That's dangerous," Scrimshaw muttered. "I mean the light. If there's holes or loose chink anywhere, they'll shoot us."

Safe, at least for the moment. But ice crystals whipped against the stubble on his face, and icy drafts sliced and eddied through his thin swallowtail, chilling him. No gloves for his numb fingers, no hat for his itching ears. Professor Figaro peered anxiously upward into an inky void. Not a hole in the overcast. Not a star, not a transparent patch of heaven. A blessing because of the total darkness, a curse of cold and snow that could kill. He'd pulled a joker, not an ace.

The road agents must have stashed horses somewhere. He needed one, especially one with a good bedroll tied behind the cantle. They'd ridden up from the south, so he started south, knowing the direction only from the gurgle of the Red Rock River. Not a good chance, he thought, knowing he could walk right past horses and not see them. He stumbled away, tripping on unseen obstacles, until the flash and crack of gunfire grew dim behind him, and the fate of his erstwhile companions vanished into the thick black night. All doomed, he thought, but he'd been ejected from the mouth of Moloch somehow, a toy of the fates. In just these moments, he'd turned numb with cold. The eddying arctic wind did it, robbing him of heat. He stumbled on, finding no sign of horses, sprawling twice. He began to shake with cold, and knew then the night would kill him if the road agents didn't. Deuces wild.

He turned around, putting the babbling river on his right, and started north, his objective the haystack. He could weather a blizzard burrowed well down into it, walling away all sight of himself. Eventually day would come, road agents would leave, and he's be rescued by a passing coach or teamsters. The shooting had stopped, and he might have walked clear past the station and its yard fronting the river but for the low, wind-whipped voices of the road agents. He turned west, groping into the blast of ice crystals toward the corrals and the stack. The snort of a horse helped, and he corrected his vector, eventually bumping hard into a corral rail, setting the ringy horses to milling and snuffling.

The corral rail proved to be a fine guide, and moments later he stumbled into the soft prickle of the stack and began to dig into the benevolent hay.

"Who the hell is that?" came a voice not ten feet away.

Professor Figaro froze. "Who the hell are you?" he retorted.

"Haze," came the reply.

The professor had his choice now. He could name a dozen names, denizens of Churchill's—but not all of them would be here. "Haze, good," he muttered. "I thought maybe Buck. Where's George?"

"On the porch. Who—"

"Listen, it's cold," said Figaro. He edged the other direction and away from warmth and shelter. No one followed.

He stood in the middle of the thick night, feeling the iced wind probe and suck and steal his heat, rob his bank. His numb left hand could barely feel the cold steel of his revolver. He knew suddenly how it was going to be for him, and he resigned himself to it.

He could think of two more possibilities, but he knew how it would end, and whatever he did, it would be like playing a game of solitaire. He might work his way to the station and knock on the door and announce his presence there. The thought amused him. He might work his way around to the rear, toward the cottonwoods, and try to locate the fool's coach and climb in. One side, at least, would be a wall of torn canvas and some protection. That amused him, too.

He felt a gust whip the swallowtails of his coat, his costume, his sporting man's attire. The remaining possibility was to sit down somewhere and freeze to death. He felt a vast emptiness. All the years of dealing cards, living out nights and sleeping days, skinning gold and greenbacks out of wily players, all of it would come to nothing.

He had a fatalistic streak, and now it gripped him. Something in his brain spoke of fate, of some giant wheel of fortune, that spun lives, spun events, and made of human will, free will, a cosmic joke. We might writhe and twist and flop like a fish on a hook, but we were hooked nonetheless. And if that was so, why fight it?

Toward his erstwhile colleagues in that coach, he felt nothing. Scrimshaw, narrow-minded and self-righteous and contemptuous of the sporting life and sporting people. The madam, Angelica, pierced now by guilt and religion, pretending she didn't do what she had spent years doing, buying her way back to respectability with the whore wages. The woman had even come to hate her fortune and was begging them all to get rid of it. For what? So she could wallow in sacrifice and appease the priests. Creed, a tower of conceit. Hayes . . . some admiration of Hayes stabbed at the gambler. But their fate would all play out, too, and no one could prevent it, stop the spin of fortune's wheel. If they died, it was ordained; if they lived, that was ordained too. . . . But his own fate grew certain to him now.

He had no inclination toward heroism. Not with a small gambler's revolver and a dozen or so road agents surrounding this station, all of them murderous and armed to the teeth. He thought a little of shooting one. He might shoot one before he himself was cut down. Find his way to that black porch, locate a hulk of humanity, and pull his trigger. But he couldn't imagine why, and it all seemed distasteful. Let fate rule.

He wandered aimlessly, circling around the station somehow, mostly by instinct, feeling the sharp wind murder him. How many lives played out well? Not one in a hundred, he thought. For the rest, the other ninety-nine, age brought broken dreams, crushed hopes, desperation, the insults of disease and injury, and relentless failure, self-hatred, disgust at ever putting plow to soil, making a marriage to an illusory human, raising children who went bad, lazy, vicious. They died, the ninety-nine out of a hundred, remembering their stupidities, their squalor, their meanness, the narrow, dull hopelessness of their miserable lives. They died remembering business failures, professional misconduct, theft and taxes, the marauding of greedy men who crowded others out, foreclosed mortgages, cut fences, trampled fields. . . . He himself was one of the ninety-nine, his life smashed by the time he was twenty-four and all the rest a somnambulant parade through the smoky salons of riverboats and mining camps, wagering fatalistically, not caring, as detached upon winning as he was upon losing.

He heard wind in naked branches and supposed he approached the cottonwoods back behind the station, though he could see nothing. If fate intended that he find the coach and shelter, he would find it.

Around him the night groaned and whistled, and he heard the creak of whipped trees. The cottonwoods. Then he tripped and tumbled over a shaft. His numb hands made out a long, thick pole with fittings at one end. A tongue. The ruined coach only feet away though he couldn't see it, creaking in the wind. He felt his way along, choosing the intact side, the one with the door.

He pulled open the door and clambered in, smelling fetid breath and rank odors of men. Too late.

Hands grabbed at him.

"Who the hell—" someone muttered. "Who's this?"

Professor Figaro sagged, stumbling over legs and arms, and settled down where no one sat.

"The professor," he said, somehow enjoying fate. "Pretty cold out there."

A lucifer scraped and whipping light dazzled his eyes, almost blinding him. But in the single second before the wind sucked away the light, he saw.

Boone Helm leering, a blued carbine light in his hands. Whiskey Bill Graves, walleyed and cadaverous and vicious. And Dutch John Wagner, thick and stolid and heavy-lidded. Of all the agents, the three worst animals.

"Evening, professor," rasped Whiskey Bill. "It ain't a fit night out, especially for wandering sports and turncoats, eh?"

Chapter Eighteen

"Bedbugs," muttered the Jehu from the bunk.

"Smoke," said Aristotle.

Unmistakable, acrid smoke drifted in the cold air.

They stood sniffing, peering into blackness.

"I can't nap anyway," said Creed.

"It's smoke," Fortitude affirmed.

A faint wavering light replaced the gloom, though its source remained invisible.

"I think the rear wall, all along the rear wall," muttered Scrimshaw. His head ached and he barely functioned.

From outside the station door, a muffled voice. "Hayes! We're through waiting. We've got a fire going along the back wall. It'll burn through. You got that long to walk out or die. Open the door, throw out the gold, and you'll live. Stay inside and you'll die."

Fortitude didn't say anything.

Angelica fell silent as granite, which surprised Aristotle.

"Could be a hoax. They don't want to burn it—too hot to get

the gold," muttered Hayes. "But I know one thing. If we walk out, we walk into gunfire. No reason to let us live as witnesses."

"Getting hotter in there, Hayes?" yelled someone.

Not hotter, Aristotle thought, but smokier. An acrid pall hung in the gloom. Pins of yellow light wormed through the chinking in the logs at several places. Not a hoax, he thought. A real fire. a last resort for the road agents. But they had a river nearby and pails anyway.

"Get me out of here. Help me out!" cried the road agent on the floor, the one called Perce.

They stood undecided in the gloom, each weighing chances and alternatives, visible to each other now in ghostly light. Briefly Hayes peered at the roof planks, splintered where the ax had pierced them, and then around the station. No ax inside—no tools. Aristotle watched him, reading his thoughts. It had come to this, he thought. Grub two years for gold, and lose it all and his life as well. He stared numbly at them all.

"Long as I'm going to die, I think I'll make it hard for them," he muttered. He picked up one of the shotguns.

"Let's organize it," muttered Hayes. "You never know."

Angelica stood solemnly, her pepperbox in one hand, somehow resigned to her fate. She said nothing at all about the wages of sin or throwing out the gold. It was too late.

From outside, a barrage of carbine fire aimed at the chinking. One ball burst through, smacking across the station, drilling a bright orange hole. The fire started to roar now, a shivering thunder along the far wall. And outside, Aristotle thought he heard hoots and cheers and laughter. Smoke coiled viciously above them and would soon drive them to the floor. He hated to die.

"Well, good-bye," he said simply. "If any of you lives—maybe you, madam—please let my, my wife—in Eagle, Wisconsin—please let her know how it . . . ended. And that I love her."

She nodded solemnly.

"You wouldn't leave me to fry in here!" cried the wounded road agent.

"Crawl," snapped Hayes.

"Had enough in there?" someone yelled.

Aristotle settled dully on the ground, where the air still tasted good. The end, then. He could scarcely fathom it, scarcely fathom the violence and shock that would rob him of life. Fast. Let it be fast, he thought. Pray. He couldn't pray. He could barely pronounce the names of Annette or his children or conjure them up in his mind this one last time. Robbery, murder, pain—all these would snare him at last, in this place far beyond law and civilization. Something like a sob burst up in him, but he choked it down.

"Still pretty dark in here, but outside the night's lit up like a torch," Fortitude droned in a strange metallic voice. "Here's what. They can't see in. They're fire-blinded. We'll swing open the shutters and door at once and start shooting. Don't run out. We'll see them out there in the firelight. Just stay inside where it's dark and shoot. They'll be blinded by all that light."

"No padre to confess to. Before we do, would you hear me, Señor Hayes?"

He nodded. She knelt, arranging her skirts with a clenched hand.

"Bless me, for I have sinned. I sell the *putas* and offend God. I am sorry. My soul, maybe it goes to hell, maybe someday something better. I won't live, but if I live . . . I will do penance for the rest of my days. Jesu Cristo, *Madre de Dios,* have mercy on me."

They waited for more, but she was done. In the faint light, Aristotle saw her making the sign of the cross over her small stout bosom.

Creed looked uncomfortable.

"Anyone else?" asked Fortitude.

No one spoke.

"Well, good-bye then," he said softly. "This is it. We all know this is it." Tears glinted on his weathered cheeks, shining in soft orange light that flamed brighter by the second. He shook hands with Creed.

"You're the best damned Jehu I ever rode the trails with, Cal. Damn, you're good. Fearless, great with the critters, makin' people feel safe. Cal Creed, you're a man. You're plumb best of all. I hope we meet again. Hope to ride messenger beside ye across the midnight skies, guardin' God's mail."

Cal Creed muttered and snuffled.

And then Aristotle felt the old man's trembling horny hand in his, pressing hard. "You're one smart workin' son of a bitch," Hayes said, his eyes bright and wet. "They can't take nothin' away from you but gold, and that ain't nothin' compared to living a fine life, grubbin' and sacrificing comforts all for the sake of that gal of yourn. She was plumb lucky to catch you, Scrimshaw, and I'd be plumb honored to shake her hand and the hands of those children of yourn. You got honor and something inside yourself that shines. We all feel the shine. I just plain knew you were square as they make 'em. Maybe we'll set around a campfire over across the divide, Aristotle, and tell tall tales."

Aristotle wept.

And then Hayes drew an arm around Angelica and squeezed her briefly.

"Been my privilege to know you, Angelica. You're a damn fine woman. Wish to blazes you wouldn't think the way you do right now. Wish you could like yourself some. I don't want you runnin' out there hating yourself. You always had a smile and poured the dust square and treated everyone right and you helped folks—slipped something to busted miners. Everyone knew that. Go to the madam and she'd stake you. I don't want you runnin' out there thinking God turned his back on you. He never does that, Angelica. He just don't do it."

A single sob convulsed her, and she gulped it back and pulled her arms around Fortitude *"Vaya con Dios,"* she whispered. "I'm glad I know you, Fortitude Hayes."

The road agent crabbed to the door, panting. "Get me outa here!"

The air turned thick; time had run out. Aristotle felt fiery smoke savage his lungs. At a nod he positioned himself at the window, ready to throw up the bar that pinned the shutters. Hayes stood ready at the door, hand on the heavy bolt. Creed stood back from the window, shotgun in hand, looking like a cigar-store Indian. Fierce heat from the rear of the building stabbed at them now, stinging necks and hands and cheeks.

Fortitude Hayes nodded and drew up the bolt, swinging open the door. Aristotle did the same, yanking open the shutters. Outside, the night ballooned with orange light. Aristotle saw no one as he swung the barrel of the shotgun. Hayes peered out, too, seeing nothing.

But they were there. Out of the wild light, lurking in the shadows and waiting. . . .

"Throw out the gold," yelled a harsh voice.

"Get it yourself!" yelled Fortitude, coughing wildly from a lungful of smoke. He peered sharply at the others. "Run!" he cried, suddenly lumbering into the night. Out in the tumbling orange, a rifle cracked in a blue flash. Hayes stumbled on his bum leg, crawled forward. Aristotle watched, paralyzed, and then followed. Carbines banged. Revolvers flashed. He heard the zip and hiss of lead. Beyond the orange lay walled dark. He sprang, some wild jolt of energy charging his body, ran hoarsely, air searing his throat and lungs. More shots. From the sides came men running, shapes racing toward the inferno, passing him. Gasping, he reached Hayes, picked him up, an arm under the shoulders, and tumbled ahead. Creed lumbered on the other side, the thick giant dragging Angelica, who puffed and struggled forward.

Someone loomed; he lifted the shotgun tucked into his arm, squeezed the cold trigger, feeling the jolt of it. Whoever loomed raced on, heading for the station.

Hayes wheezed in his grip, cursing slowly, profaning the night, coughing and sputtering.

"They're gold-crazy," he wheezed. "They'll take care of us later. Let's git while we can."

So that was it! Aristotle marveled that he lived, that his brain worked, that blood coursed in his arteries. They reached the river, halting suddenly at the ford. They gaped at each other, gasping for air, stared unbelieving in the shivering amber light, sweated up and trembling—and cold, as ice chips from the lowering clouds stung them.

Behind, in the distant station, they saw the dark bulks of busy men, their faces covered with bandanas, dragging heavy black objects into the night, valises, saddlebags, half a ton of stolen gold. Hayes wheezed desperately, as if his lungs had given out. Creed stared stolidly at the frantic work at the station.

"Wish I had the Sharps," he muttered.

Angelica panted and began to sob.

Hayes tried to talk but couldn't manage. Then he gasped. "We got to hide. Once they got the gold, they'll come. Horses," he said. "Look for Figaro."

That was all he could manage, and he wheezed again, panting.

"They rode up from the south," Aristotle muttered.

They turned right, up the riverbank. The light faded swiftly. Blackness crowded ahead, a blank wall. Aristotle glared behind, watching the road agents drag out more valises. The injured one crawled through the orange-lit doorway, unaided by gold-mad robbers. Sparks coiled into the night, whipped by the iced wind. A rear log, or the wall itself, collapsed, piling a star shower into the indigo.

He felt nothing. No sense of deliverance, for they weren't delivered, and the road agents would hunt them down for the slaughter in moments. His body trembled and threatened to collapse under him. No food, no sleep. And the threat of death, of pain and torture, of all the malign powers of evil swarming over him. And now the weight of Fortitude Hayes, who could limp no farther.

They stumbled through night, with only a faint yellow glow shining from the bellies of low black clouds behind them for guidance. That and the rippling river. A horse snorted somewhere in the dark.

Fortitude Hayes, staggering beside him, heard it and began cackling. Mad, Aristotle thought. Plumb mad. The old sergeant sounded like a gathering of wolves.

* * *

Dirty hands dug and pawed at Professor Figaro, yanking his small revolver from him, the hideout derringer, the light poke, the billfold in the right breast pocket of his swallowtail, and its cargo of five hundred dollars in Union greenbacks, two decks of virgin playing cards, locket and tintype, and the headlight diamond stickpin in his cravat.

Whiskey Bill struck another lucifer. "What's this?" he said, eyeing first the tintype of Figaro's parents, stiffly posed, and then the beautiful face in the porcelain miniature. "A girly. You pick 'em and stick 'em, perfessor."

Bereft. Randolph Figaro sagged back against the coach wall fatalistically. He entertained no hopes. The cards had played out, and there remained only the chips on the board. He could see the three others now: the whole rear wall of the way station burned brightly, amber flames whipped by a north wind, crawling up the logs, eating wood, flaring along eaves.

The eerie light played like a devil's lantern across Whiskey Bill's face, probing into his puckered mouth with its stained, twisted teeth and gummy gaps. Over in the black shadow across the coach slumped Boone Helm, agate-eyed, radiating animal murder and stinking with sweated booze. And even deeper in the wavering darkness, Dutch John Wagner, thick and rheumy, heavy-lidded as a Dutch oven, an idiot smirk pasted to his wattled face.

"Should have joined the crowd, professor," said Boone Helm, grinning. "You lost. That fire'll drive the pilgrims out and it'll be all over. You could have had a share."

"I've always played a square game," said Figaro softly.

Dutch John Wagner chortled, a pig's giggle.

Figaro glanced idly through the coach window at the inferno. And toward the road agents poised in shadow to slaughter anyone who burst out. He felt oddly empty and calm, and waited his fate hollowly. Nothing whined or cowered and wept inside of him, and an amiable emptiness filtered through his mind. Better than screaming terror, he thought. It came from understanding fate.

"How does it feel to die, professor?" asked Whiskey Bill.

"A good question. About the same as living, I suppose."

"You a southerner? I think you are."

"Mississippi."

"We're all Rebs," said Helm. "Mostly, anyway. Not Ives or Plummer."

"How come you ain't squirming and crying? Maybe I should stick you a little," said Dutch John.

"I kneel before Lady Luck."

"I don't get that. You don't believe in heaven and hell and all that?"

"I was a sporting man."

"Was." Dutch John chortled.

"Who's this in the locket?" asked Whiskey Bill Graves.

"Someone better than me."

"Gimme a name, goddammit. Maybe I'll send it to her for you."

"I killed her."

That subdued them. The professor doubted that any of these roughs had murdered a woman. They peered at him in the dancing light with strange respect.

"You killed her?" echoed Helm. He plucked the locket from Whiskey Bill's hands and held it up to the light. "Hell," he said, a grudging admiration in his face. "You're a tough one, Figaro. Yes sir. Shot her?"

"Shot her," said Randolph Figaro blandly. "Through the breast."

"Lemme see," rasped Dutch John. He snatched the locket and peered with heavy-lidded wonderment. "I'd want to use her first. Did you use her first?"

"No," said Figaro

"I'd use her a few times first."

Out in the yellow night, shouts and shots erupted above the roar of the fire.

"They're coming out. Got to go help now, Figaro." He leered. "You could always try running and tempt fate, Figaro."

The three of them clambered out of the groaning coach, cursing at its tilt, and dashed toward the station. Figaro sat bewildered on the slanting floor, suddenly granted a brief stay of execution. He couldn't see much. From the tilted coach he could see only the blazing rear of the station, and all the murder and mayhem would be at its front, around the door and window. He thought to run out into the icy night, and set the thought aside. Fate had played out the last card, so why resist?

He settled back into the coach, discovering a tarpaulin that one of the road agents had abandoned. He wrapped it around his numb body and quickly felt better, all in favor of comfort while they collected their chips.

It amused him, their sudden respect. Not even these road agents could boast of a crime so terrible as his own. He watched events play out around the station, understanding almost none of it. Blurred shapes racing into the gloom, others running toward the station. Dark figures dragging heavy things—the valises full of gold. The rear portion of the station collapsed with a roar, geysering up a shower of embers.

He idled away the moment pondering fate. Odd, he thought. He should be dead. Not forty-eight hours ago he'd been defying fate for all he was worth, plotting his escape from Churchill's, meeting with Hayes, setting a time and place. Using his will and intelligence to spit at fate. Life meant something to him then, only hours ago. Why not now? Why did he wait here in this fool's coach, wait for fate's revolver to discharge?

He had no answer, but sensed some profound anomaly inside of himself, as if he were two people—one alive and struggling and wrestling to make a better life, the other resigned and passive, the gambler self, knowing that the cards fell as they fell, making winners and losers of us all. It startled him to see two separate characters within himself, passive and active, caring and uncaring, defiant and fatalistic, willful and submissive. He suddenly loathed gambling and the mood it cast upon him. If he lived, he would make himself something else. Good-bye to the sporting life, the watershot-silk vest and swallowtail, the smoky salons, the green baize, the cold calculation, skinning sustenance from the fall of deuces and aces. Could all these years of subservience to fate have been nothing but a way of punishing himself for an unintended murder? Had he murdered his own will because he had murdered the woman he loved? Was his frenzied effort to escape Churchill's, to live, something good and true within himself? Yes! Why be the slave of fate when he'd been born with will and purpose? He stirred, some excitement stealing through him.

It all astonished him as much as being alive at this point astonished him. He took swift inventory: Not a weapon left to him. No boots or mittens or cap—but a solid tarpaulin against the cold. No horse, no food. But he was hard upon a well-traveled road. No greenbacks, no cards. But five thousand in dust still in Dance's safe, ready for use when it could be gotten safely out of the Alder district.

Astonished, he stirred in the fool's coach, suddenly wanting to live. Hide in the night. Hope he left no footprints in the skim of snow. Hunt for a horse. Go off into the indigo and live. He opened the coach door and stepped out into bitter air.

Chapter Nineteen

At the edge of blackness they stood, watching the whirling blaze consume the way station. Yellow light caromed off the bellies of low clouds, making the night eerie with wavering, bilious rays. They could flee no farther; they could not will another step from trembling legs.

Angelica thought her heart would burst. She clung to Cal Creed, leaning heavily upon his massive body. Beside them, Aristotle Scrimshaw held Fortitude Hayes upright, an arm under his shoulders.

They'd missed the horses, raced too far into the black river flats. The road agents had tied their horses on the far side of the corrals all in a row, and now Angelica and the others watched helplessly as shadowed figures, silhouetted in the firelight, led the animals toward the humped mass of valises they'd dragged from the station.

Over the crackle of the wildfire, they heard laughter and hooting. One by one the night riders mounted, each with with a heavy valise nestled in his lap. Angelica watched coldly as her six bags, her fortune, were hoisted to riders. They didn't know what to do with Scrimshaw's heavier saddlebags, and some of them wandered to the pens, studied the wounded harness horses, and returned to the yard. The station porch was ablaze now, lighting them all distinctly.

"Maybe they'll ditch your saddlebags, Scrimshaw," muttered Creed. "Two hundred pounds."

But even as he spoke, a tow-haired road agent began slicing the leather in two, separating the pair of bags. In a moment he hoisted a severed bag to a rider. Angelica glanced at Aristotle, who watched grimly, exhaustion etched in every granite line of his young face.

At the last, the road agents made a rough splint for their injured man and helped him up. One of them turned his horse away and rode toward them, his hair glinting yellow but his face lost in black shadow. He stopped well out of shotgun range.

"We know you're there," he yelled. "Git out of the country. We see any of you again, you're dead."

For an answer, Creed lifted the shotgun and fired, the blast sharp in the night.

The road agent laughed, wheeled his horse and trotted back to the others.

"Bluff," Cal snorted. "They got what they wanted and don't want to tangle with our shotguns. We got the dark behind us; they ain't."

But Angelica wasn't listening. She watched the road agents ride their horses off to the north, each carrying a piece of her life, watched them disappear into the blackness of the cottonwoods, past the faint glint of the fool's coach parked there. The shots surprised her. As they passed the dim-lit coach, they emptied their revolvers into it, and she heard their fading laughter as they vanished into the night.

Then it grew silent, save for the crackle of the subdued fire, feeding now on foundation logs. She heard the ripple of the Red Rock River, and felt again the spit of ice from the sky. She lived, and found herself faintly surprised and pleased.

"We'll just wait awhile before going back there," muttered Fortitude, who sounded less winded. "Sitting ducks."

Cold air sucked at her and drove about her legs and down her neck. But she stood rooted, safe in the shelter of blackness. Everything gone. Maybe not everything. In the fading light she thought she made out the remaining valise, her clothing and personal things, scattered in the yard. And beyond it, Scrimshaw's traveling bag, too.

"Hate to go back," muttered Hayes. "We'll find the professor in the coach. That's what that was all about. Tied up in there and plumb dead. A good man. Glad I knew him. Had something right about him, crooked smile and square heart."

"Afraid you're right," said Aristotle in a weary voice. "They got him. They killed him for knowing too much."

"I don't know why I'm alive," said Angelica. "I don't know why. The sporting man—he should be alive, not me."

"Consarn it, Angelica," muttered Hayes.

They began to drift back to the station, impelled by weariness and the promise of warmth, all of them ready to ignore the possibility of a lingering sniper.

"Shouldn't do this," Hayes muttered, limping ahead with the help of Aristotle. "Suicide."

But they trudged ahead anyway.

They passed the corrals. One horse sprawled in the manure, yellow light glistening from its belly. Two others stood, one alert, the other braced and low, fighting collapse.

"Feed the good horse. Hay the good horse," Fortitude muttered.

Creed let go of her and walked toward the hay pile. It surprised her that the Jehu would do it without protest.

"Good evening, Creed," came a soft voice from the shadowed foot of the stack.

The Jehu snapped up, lifted his shotgun and fired, the blast booming through darkness.

Laughter. "A little lower and you would have got me, Cal," came the familiar voice. Professor Figaro unfolded slowly, looking strange in a canvas poncho.

"You live!" cried Angelica. She sobbed, ran forward and threw her arms about the sporting man, hugging hard, feeling her tears on her cheeks.

"You are here. We thought you—*muerto,* dead."

"So did I," replied the professor, hugging her tight.

"Be damned," muttered Hayes, wobbling toward the man.

Creed attempted to apologize. "Little touchy still, little touchy. Glad I missed."

Fortitude glared at him. "Reload," he snapped. "Git out and watch sharp. Hay them horses."

"They thought I was still in the coach," said the professor. "That's where they left me talking about fate. Dutch John Wagner, Whiskey Bill, and Boone Helm."

"You are alive!" she exclaimed. "I prayed for your soul. Only a little time in purgatory, I asked for that. For you. Only a little time."

"Alive for the moment," he replied. "I know too much."

"Git outa this light. Plumb crazy," Hayes snapped.

"Soon," said Figaro.

They gathered before the glowing station, enjoying its warmth, feeling its dying comfort. Angelica tried to imagine life in deep poverty, and couldn't. The future lay blank as this night. In the waning light, she found her broken bag, her few things yanked from it and scattered across raw earth, silky things, a traveling suit, comb and brush, the two tintypes of her boys, Jaime and Carlos. . . .

She picked them up from the packed earth, feeling the warmth of the blaze in them still. Swiftly, she pulled at the backing, tugged at soft cardboard, and found the greenbacks intact. Six thousand dollars. Six thousand in grubby green bank notes!

She slumped to the warm earth, choked and shivering.

"Angelica. You all right?" muttered Fortitude, who stood trembling on his weak leg above her.

She nodded, speechless, nodded and smiled softly.

"Them your family? Your sons?"

She nodded, mute. It would be a start. All she needed, really.

But sin-money, sin-money. . . . A great sadness filled her. These dirty notes had come from the *putas,* from the business, from what she'd been. Burn them. Pull them out and throw them into the flames of hell! How could she? How could she have hidden dirty money behind the images of her two innocent *hijos*? Tears welled again, and she slumped into the earth, too exhausted to think.

Nearby, young Scrimshaw picked up his few possessions, scattered around his ransacked traveling portmanteau, and slumped wearily to earth.

"Nothing left," he muttered to her. "We'll have to start over. I've lost the farm now, and God knows, maybe my boy—he needs a doctor who knows something about consumption."

"Señor Scrimshaw. We're alive," she said in a small voice.

He smiled thinly. "I've never thought much about death," he replied. "Not until tonight, anyway."

She fell silent. Something within her felt buoyant and light, and she recognized it. The gold no longer weighed upon her, crushing her soul, tormenting her. She felt feathery and free. Let the road agents have the wages of sin. For years she had pushed aside all thought of sin, of good and evil, of stained gold, but the moment she prepared for this trip, for her new life, the thoughts crept into her mind unbidden. All the while, as she and Alfonso prepared, the small, silent voice was telling her that she could be outwardly respectable, outwardly a rich widow, but inwardly never. She might live her days out in San Francisco in comfort and privacy, her secret hidden darkly in her heart, but the life would be a sad one, and her days bitter and discontented.

But now, sitting on the raw earth in her expensive traveling suit, she felt giddy with release. They'd taken hell from her and run off with it. She liked her nakedness. *Madre de Dios,* see me now, she thought. See me now, giddy as a girl dancing in a summer meadow. They took hell away, but now I give it away also, this evil gold. I will not grieve the loss because it's no loss.

She frowned. For there still remained a corner of hell wrapped tightly in butcher paper behind the innocent images of two lost sons. She must surrender that, too—everything!

Hungry but no food. Tired but no rest. Warm at least, lying on the heated clay. Alive. A fortune gone. His careful plan, the resurrected coach, a failure, foolishness. He'd stopped blaming himself for the snapped thoroughbrace. It hadn't made any difference, not after the fight at Red Rock station. He thought of getting a horse and pursuing them all, a silent avenger, assassinating them one by one in the night, revenge in his cold, hard heart. But he felt too tired for anger, too tired for anything but escape. He'd have to work his way east while Annette waited months more, no doubt evicted and huddled somewhere.

All gone, the prize of brutal labor through heavy cold and hard heat, honest toil. He chided himself only for greed, and wished he'd folded things up months earlier, content with enough rather than grasping for a Midas fortune. Peabody and Caldwell owed him passage to Fort Hall. Beyond that . . . blankness. He couldn't think anyway, and slid swiftly toward oblivion.

Hayes shook him. "I've been digging a hole in the stack," he said. "This is no place here; it'll cool down soon and you'll freeze plumb to death. Safer there, too—from varmints with guns."

"Leave me be," muttered Aristotle.

But Hayes kicked and bullied him until he stumbled over to the stack and fell into a nest of hay. Someone beside him pulled a tarp over him and he fell instantly asleep, curiously warm in the nest of dry grass. They all slept, too worn to set a guard.

The sun stood high when he awoke, and he discovered he was the last to waken. Starved. Famished. Dizzy. He kicked loose the tarpaulin and stood up in a clear, cold morning with a heatless sun promising nothing for comfort. Before his blinking eyes, a wagon stood, and the one unscathed dray hunched in harness.

Fortitude Hayes grinned. "You sawed a lot of wood," he said. "This here Peabody and Caldwell conveyance is about to depart for points south, Creed driving, Hayes the messenger."

Aristotle found no humor in anything. "We could be thinking about getting my gold back," he snapped.

Hayes's eyes went bright. "We could just do that," he replied acidly. "Yes, we could."

Aristotle didn't feel like facing the morning. The full weight of the tragedy crushed his soul and numbed his body. "You go on without me," he said. "I'm going to sleep some more."

"Climb into the haystack and die," Fortitude said gently. "I suppose I would, too, if'n I had a fortune stole away."

Aristotle hadn't expected sympathy from the crabbed old sergeant, and stared, wondering if the man was ridiculing him.

"There's not much justice in the world, Scrimshaw. A man like you grubs and mucks an honest fortune, and some bandits and scum of the earth snatch it all away. World always was like that—not much justice. There's no promise that virtue's going to be rewarded and wickedness is going to be punished. No, that's just a kind of blind hope we all got, but it don't fit the facts none. But most folks are honest enough, and most towns are pretty nice places to live."

Aristotle didn't want a lecture. Not this morning. Not when he felt bereft and naked and starved and almost two thousand miles from his family and the future a blank, and . . .

Fortitude hawked and spat. "No telling about fate," he continued. "Blasted minié ball smashes up my knee, and next thing I know I'm discharged and I no longer got a career and not much of a pension, and I got no chance to lead men to their glory or win more stripes. Naw, no glory in having a bum knee. But I ain't pushing up daisies either, Scrimshaw. Naw, unjust fate saw to that. Damned if I ain't alive and well and blasting away at bandits every other coach run."

"You're telling me I should be glad to be alive. Life is everything."

Hayes stood silently.

Aristotle didn't feel any joy in living. He stood, feeling body and soul sag within him.

"Git on to the river and wash your face. And stand like a man, Scrimshaw. Get on with living."

But Aristotle saw the shotgun messenger through blurred eyes. The tears he hated welled up like hot lava, unbidden, and his body convulsed. All that hard work . . . all his hopes . . . all his caring for Annette and the children . . . all his bright, shining dreams. . . . He sobbed and folded into the raw earth, burying his wet face in his thick, hard hands.

He saw the shape of the future. He'd work his way home, wherever home might be after the bank foreclosed. He'd enter the door with nothing in his hands and the lines of defeat graven upon his face. He'd watch Annette read his face, see his empty hands and worn clothes. He'd hug her then, feeling her stiffness and disappointment—and her contempt. Feel her grow distant and alien and bitter, never to return to him, never to care. He'd see Thompson, his dying son, lying weak and disappointed and hopeless in his blanket. Only Margaret would smile, and she not for long. He'd lose them, lose their love and respect, and live out his days a branded man, the weak one, the fool, the dreamer, the visionary who let a farm die and a family collapse while he chased the rainbow. . . .

He felt everything crumble away within him, the last vestiges of manhood and courage, of dignity and pride. Whatever he had been, it was gone. The things he'd treasured, his strength and courage, his willingness to persevere, his integrity, the love he carried in the vessel of his soul for his family, for God, for a good world, for a new way of living in a new world, for his belief in goodness . . . all gone. And at the bottom of this terrible despair he saw nothing at all, his own dead soul, a bitter and alien wife, a dead son, a pinched landless life, a hired man's grim toil.

He felt at last small feminine hands slipping gently over his shoulders and arms, the hands of a madam, a woman who had owned a parlor house and sold lust. He felt her hands comforting him, this Magdalen, and heard her soft cooing beside him.

"Señor Scrimshaw, it goes hard, no?"

He didn't want to respond. He wanted to bury himself. But her hands tugged and fluttered about him there on cold earth.

"What will we do now, Señor Scrimshaw, throw life away now? I'm not going to. You—you have something that I don't. You have good reason to be proud. Nothing to be ashamed of. Me, I am ashamed."

Something eased within him, and he no longer felt his body convulse and choke.

"I was married once—to an older man, a don, very rich and very cruel, who—*Dios,* he bruised me and I wept away my days until I couldn't weep anymore, and all I had inside, like a volcano, was hot lava and hatred. I ran away. It was run away or kill him. That's when I shut out what was good and began the life I lived. I told myself I had no choice. What was a woman to do, a woman who ran away? So hard. My soul turned to rock. And for all this time I was stone. Before God, I have much to answer for. But you have little to answer for, Señor Scrimshaw. You can stand up right now, you can stand up in this morning sun, possessing nothing, stand up and be glad of life, be glad of the *esposa*—the wife and the little ones. Stand up and be glad for the day, for the hour, for the water in the river that you drink, and the air you breathe. It is nothing, the gifts of God—and it is everything, this beat of the heart in your chest."

He felt her hands caressing, willing strength into him, and he took them into his own.

"I have something, Señor Scrimshaw," she said. "They missed something of mine. Some greenbacks hidden in the tintypes of my Jaime and Carlos, my *hijos.* . . . I give it to you. Some for the others, too. Something for Professor Figaro, because he has nothing, either. Something for Señor Hayes and Señor Creed, who risked their lives for us. I give it all away now. Six thousand dollars."

He stared, astonished. "I could use the fare back to Wisconsin. I'll pay you back as soon as—"

"Madre de Dios!" she scolded.

He understood then that he was rejecting her gift, making it a loan, letting his pride rule him again. "Whatever you give, I'm grateful to have," he muttered.

From above him, he heard the professor. "I have dust in Dance's safe. It can't be gotten out now, but sometime the roads will be cleared of these bandits, and then I'll be fine."

"Take something, professor. You need something while you wait. I want you to take—a thousand."

"You are kind, Angelica. I won't ever forget."

"Me and Creed—we're just on duty, Angelica," said Hayes. "We're not lookin' for anything except to run the stages safe and fast."

"A thousand is yours. For each."

"Naw," said Creed.

"Take it! I need only a little to travel with," she replied. "Take it!"

But they wouldn't. Aristotle accepted five hundred dollars gratefully. Enough for the Overland stage, and rail fare. The professor accepted five hundred as well, to tide him over.

Aristotle stood, calm and drained of rage and tears, and hugged the small woman, thanking her.

"Let's get rolling," yelled Creed. "This coach is heading for Pine Butte, Pleasant Valley, Camas Creek, Eagle Rock, and Fort Hall. Transferring at Fort Hall to points east and west."

Chapter Twenty

He arrived on Christmas Day and found them still in their sturdy farm home, gaily decorated with pine garlands and red ribbons. The Husbandmen's Bank had not yet evicted them.

Annette gasped and cried when he appeared, and he did not feel the stiffness and resistance when he drew her joyously into his strong arms and hugged.

"What a Christmas gift!" she cried, laughing and sobbing and altogether beside herself.

Margaret danced and pirouetted and tugged at his big hand, and Thompson, waxen-faced and cadaverous, grinned feverishly from the settee where he sat wrapped in a quilt.

He told her about the gold.

"I knew it would be like that, Aristotle," she said, always the pessimist. "But what does it matter? You're here! Is there anything more to ask for?"

Had she loved him so much, that all she needed was his presence? He'd been a fool, on a fool's errand.

He sat beside his son, heart aching at the sight of so much disease torturing the small young body.

"You really had a hundred thousand dollars of gold?" the boy asked, awed.

"I did, before the road agents stole it."

"That's more money than I ever heard of."

"I'm told it was the most any miner grubbed out of Alder Gulch, Thompson."

"You're the best father that ever was," the boy said, his eyes full of admiration. "I bet you're the only pap in all the world that got so much gold."

Aristotle laughed. "Lots of men win more and own great mines, Thompson. But I dug a lot, all right."

He caught Annette later, beside the kitchen stove. "I'm sorry," he said.

"For what, Aristotle? You tried. For us. And now this is the best Christmas we've ever had."

It took a number of inquiries, but at last Randolph Figaro got directions to the recruitment office outside of Denver City, near the bivouac of the Colorado Volunteers. He rented a buggy and drove there and presented himself to a stocky, florid major in a tight blue uniform.

"I was born in Mississippi, but I wish to volunteer for service to the North," he said. "I imagine I'm too old for combat, but I have long experience in import-export and freight forwarding. I could help with the quartermaster work in any capacity."

"You're obviously a gambler," the major growled.

"I was that."

"Quartermaster work. Nice spot for a Reb spy to report on our logistics," the major snapped. "Nice place for a tinhorn gambler to use a little sleight of hand and clean us out."

"You will have my oath, on my honor, sir. . . ."

"Any Reb can make an oath."

He felt his chances slipping. "You have my offer, sir, given squarely."

The major sighed, tugged at his thick walrus mustache. "I think not. No tinhorns and no Rebs. I'm putting your name down, Figaro. If we catch you spying again, we'll put you before the firing squad."

He left, feeling his birthplace and his profession upon him, and knowing of no escape. He drifted on down to the wild town of Pueblo, relishing its warmth after the cold of Idaho. There he kept cases at a faro layout owned by Julius Dugg, and sometimes dealt, letting the days slip by.

He wrote Dance, asking that his gold be shipped express as soon as it was safe to do so. Dance never replied, and after six months Professor Figaro knew he wouldn't see the pokes again. The merchant probably joined the vigilantes the professor had heard about, and had confiscated the dust.

He lacked the bank to run his own game, or even buy a layout, but playing skillful poker in odd hours he began to build a small nest egg, week by week. He was trapped by what he was, he thought, but he'd make the best of it. In a few months, if his poker luck held, he'd be back in business, with his crooked smile and square game. It would be enough, he thought. He enjoyed life and found small pleasures to buoy him along, including increasing amounts of bourbon.

She bought coach fare to Denver City via Julesburg, and then fare to Santa Fe, finding a room at a low adobe called La Fonda. Down the street the beginnings of a great cathedral surprised her, but otherwise the dun city seemed as austere and sweet as always, with the incense of piñon pine from a thousand beehive fireplaces and stoves hovering over it.

She didn't know what she would do. She might starve to death. But first things first. She felt weary, but she had a journey to make. She thought to walk, as a kind of penance, and after washing her face and pummeling the road dust from her black suit, she trudged toward the beautiful mission church, San Miguel, passing through narrow streets in the low amber light of early December, the Advent season. At the heavy door of the church, she paused, frightened, and then slipped in. She paused before the altar with its guttering tabernacle candle guarding the Host, and curtsied, and then laid before the altar a thin packet and proceeded to the dark box at the rear, hoping a padre would be there. Usually they were at this hour.

She entered, drew the curtain behind her, and knelt, trembling with fear. Behind the grille a priest waited.

"Bless me, Father, for I have sinned," she began, reciting the ancient ritual. Then with tears and trembling she started at the beginning and told her story, stumbling on for an hour, into the cold lavender twilight that caught the lovely city in its unearthly web. Then she waited. Unforgiveness? No, not that. God would forgive. But a burden of penance she would bear as best she could for as long as she had breath.

The hidden priest remained silent a long time, and she felt raw fear.

"Your husband died long ago, Señora Ramirez, unrepentant and without the sacraments of the Church, excommunicated by Bishop Lamy. Your sons looked for you and spread word everywhere. They heard ugly rumors, but found no sign of you. You had your widow's portion coming, and it still exists, the *casa* and a modest income. Carlos married happily, though his heart is often heavy with longing for his missing mother. Your other son, Jaime, became a priest. . . ."

She knelt, choked and trembling.

"Ego te absolvo," said the priest. "You are forgiven."

She waited. "There is no penance?"

"What does our Lord require of thee but a broken and contrite heart?" said the priest.

She wept.

"I will take you home, *madre,*" he said.

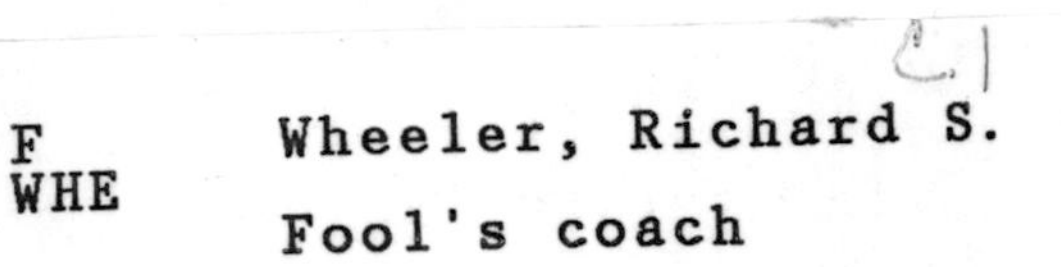